DOCTOR·WHO

The Nightmare of Black Island

Collect all the exciting new Doctor Who *adventures*:

DOCTOR·WHO

The
Nightmare
of
Black Island

BY MIKE TUCKER

BBC
BOOKS

Published by BBC Books, BBC Worldwide Ltd,
Woodlands, 80 Wood Lane, London W12 0TT

First published 2006
10 9 8 7 6 5

Commissioning Editor: Stuart Cooper
Creative Director and Editor: Justin Richards
Production Controller: Peter Hunt

Doctor Who is a BBC Wales production for BBC ONE
Executive Producers: Russell T Davies and Julie Gardner
Producer: Phil Collinson

Cover design by Henry Steadman © BBC 2006
Typeset in Albertina by Rocket Editorial Ltd, Aylesbury, Bucks
Printed and bound in Great Britain by
Cox & Wyman Ltd, Reading, Berkshire

For more information about this and other BBC books,
please visit our website at www.bbcshop.com

For Karen

The first clap of thunder echoed off the cliff face like cannon fire, sending gulls shrieking into the dark, brooding sky. Out across the waves a bright fork of lightning lit up the purple clouds on the horizon and, with another ominous rumble of thunder, the rain swept in from the sea.

Carl Jenkins looked up in despair and struggled with the hood of his jacket as a sharp gust of wind swirled the rain around him. He glowered angrily at the sky as the rain became a torrent, and cursed his luck.

The weather had been against him almost as soon as he set out on this holiday. When he left his flat in Bristol the sun had been shining and his spirits had been high. He should have known that his fortunes were going to change as soon as he saw the boiling clouds on the other side of the Severn Bridge. It was typical. Every trip he made into Wales was the same.

Paying the toll was like putting coins into a launderette washing machine: no sooner had they clunked into the slot than the water started to pour.

The brochure advertising holidays in west Wales that had fallen out of his local newspaper had seemed ideal. The photographs of the bays and cliff tops looked idyllic, but it had been a paragraph about the fishing that had finally convinced Carl to pick up the phone and book.

His father had been a great fisherman. Old family holidays had always started with a regular routine of unpacking long canvas bags from the attic, checking rods and reels, sprucing up floats. The entire exercise fascinated Carl and there had always been that extra thrill of danger when his father untied the small pouch filled with gleaming hooks, pointing out sternly that they were not to be touched under any circumstances.

Not that he would have gone anywhere near them. The wicked barbs on the tips had terrified him and he had always curled his hands into fists so that there was no chance one of those metal spikes could get near his fingers.

Carl had spent a pleasant couple of hours pulling his father's rods and bags from the attic and checking that everything was in working order. It came as some surprise to find that the bag of hooks still sent a familiar chill down his spine, and he found himself smiling at how stupid childhood memories continued to have such a strong influence.

Ynys Du had seemed like an ideal spot. The village was small and pretty with a couple of decent pubs, the campsite was only a few minutes' walk from the centre and the brochure had pointed out several good spots for fishing along the coast. There was even a disused lighthouse on the island out in the bay – a ragged lump of black rock that explained the name of the village – and the photographs in the brochure had given the entire area a picture-postcard feel.

The truth was that now, under the dark and brooding sky that had loomed low overhead ever since his arrival, the village had a completely different feel. The long, tangled line of rocks along the coast that looked so pretty in the sunlight had taken on a harsh, jagged feel, the waves boiling angrily along their edge sending spray high into the air. On top of all that, the campsite was deserted, his little orange tent the only one. He hadn't even been able to get hold of the site owner.

Carl shivered inside his jacket. The rain was icy cold and the wind was starting to cut right through him. He glanced back along the coast at the village. As the rain soaked into the stone of the buildings, the entire village seemed to darken and solidify, becoming cold and unfriendly. Another loud crack of thunder made him jump. It suddenly seemed like a very long walk back to the relative comfort of his tent, and he was aware of how treacherous the paths along the cliffs were becoming as they started to stream with water.

With a deep sigh, he started to reel in his line, wincing as lightning arced across the waves. The lighthouse that had been so picturesque in the brochure now stood out like a dark, ominous spire in the water, the black rocks at its base flecked with foam from the raging ocean.

A sudden flare of pale light made Carl glance up, puzzled. That hadn't been lightning. He brushed away the stray strands of hair that had matted themselves across his face and peered through the lashing rain at the looming shape of the island in the bay. Surely that flash had come from the lighthouse…

As he struggled to see through the rainwater stinging his face, another faint pulse of light lit up the clouds. It *had* come from the lighthouse! He could see a faint flicker of sickly green-grey light from the lamp room. He frowned. The lighthouse was meant to be deserted; it was a relic from the days when Ynys Du had been a busy mining community and ships had had to pick their way through the treacherous sandbanks that lay just off the coast. According to the guidebook, it hadn't been used since the 1970s.

He reached for one of the canvas bags at his side. His binoculars were tucked into a leather case in there, packed with the fishing gear in case there was an opportunity for bird-watching. Shaking the rain from his eyes, Carl groped around in the sodden bag. He gave a sudden cry as he felt a searing pain.

He whipped his hand back from the bag, tears of agony welling in his eyes, struggling not to let the rod clatter down the rocks and into the swirling sea. Blood streamed down his hand, diluted by the lashing rain, and he could see the gleaming end of one of the fishhooks protruding through the tip of his thumb.

Stumbling to his feet, Carl tried to wedge the rod under his arm, turning his back to the wind and pulling at the hook. He felt sick and dizzy. All the nightmares about fishhooks that he had had as a kid suddenly threatened to overwhelm him. The hook was buried quite deep and there was no way he was going to be able to just pull it free without tearing out a good portion of his flesh with it.

His stomach heaved and for a moment he thought he might faint. He tried to slow his breathing. He was being stupid. It was just a fishhook, for God's sake. He was a grown man, not a frightened kid. He had a pair of pliers back in the car. All he had to do was snip off the barb and the rest of the hook would slide out easily. The cold was already numbing his hand, dulling the pain. He tried to wipe the blood from his palm, fumbling in his pocket for a handkerchief.

Then two things happened at once: a child's laughter, shockingly close, made him stumble back in alarm, and at the same time the rod jerked in his arms, bending sharply as something heavy hauled on the line. Carl struggled to keep his footing on the rain-slick grass as the tug on the rod became an insistent pressure, the reel spinning uncontrollably. The laughter came again and a tiny shape appeared out of the rain. A small child, a young boy no more than five years old, dressed in flannel pyjamas and clutching a bedraggled soft toy, stared at him through the downpour, seemingly unaware of the biting wind. The boy raised a pale hand, pointed at Carl and giggled, the wind swirling the sound eerily across the cliff tops.

Carl felt a sudden chill of fear as he realised that the child wasn't pointing at him but past him, at something in the water. The line continued to unwind wildly, the noise from the reel now a high-pitched scream. As Carl started to turn, the rod was wrenched violently from his grip, sending him sprawling.

With a guttural, bubbling roar, something vast and glistening emerged from the raging ocean. Carl stared in disbelief as the thing clawed its way up the rocks, waves breaking on its broad back. It was huge, well over two metres tall, its skin a mass of barnacle-covered heavy plates and iridescent scales, a patchwork of different bright colours altogether too gaudy for any creature Carl had ever seen. Its head was squat and crested, with spines emerging directly from its shoulders. The jaw worked spasmodically, as if struggling to draw breath, and its eyes glowed a deep fiery red. It hauled itself over the rocks with four powerfully muscled arms, claws gouging out great lumps as it came.

The red eyes fixed on him and the creature threw back its head and gave a bellowing roar. Bright tongues of flame burned in its throat, as if at its centre was a vast ball of fire. Steam hissed around it as the rain boiled on its skin. Carl started to scrabble away, but the creature bounded forward, looming over him, shrieking in triumph.

As it raised one huge paw in the air, Carl realised with horror that its claws were barbed and metallic, like fishhooks. He closed his eyes as the huge arm swept down and was suddenly aware of a sharp pain, and then there was nothing but the sound of rain, and sea, and the laughter of a small child, slowly fading.

Way out in the depths of space, the police box shell of the TARDIS appeared in a blaze of blue light, tumbling end over end in the dark. It spun for a moment, as if getting its bearings, and then, with a swirling kaleidoscope of shimmering colour flaring around it, vanished again into the time vortex.

Inside the Doctor sat cross-legged on the floor, poking and prodding at the tangle of tubes and pipes that wound their way through the coral-like growths and protuberances of the central control console. Above him the huge glass and crystal column of the time rotor rose and fell in steady progression, keeping time like the tick of a huge clock, or the beat of a heart.

The lights in the console room were dim and low, the huge curving walls in shadow, the indented roundels glowing softly with emerald light. Rose was curled up on the battered control room chair, the Doctor's long brown coat draped over her like a blanket. She was fast asleep, her breathing slow and measured, keeping pace with the rotor.

The Doctor peered round the console at her, smiling. It was rare to see her so quiet and still; she was usually such a bundle of tireless energy, always keen to head off to the next great adventure, to find somewhere new to explore.

The steady background hum from the console suddenly changed in pitch for a moment and there was a faint moan from Rose as she stirred on the chair. The Doctor frowned and clambered to his feet, peering at a flashing light on the console.

'Well, that's not right… Not right at all.'

He pulled a pair of thick-rimmed glasses from his jacket pocket and leaned forward, his nose almost brushing the controls. He tapped at a read-out.

'What are you flashing for? You're not meant to flash. If I'd wanted you to flash I'd have put you somewhere more obvious, more flashy.'

There was another bleep from the other side of the console. The Doctor hurried around to where a new set of lights had blinked into life, twisting controls as he went. A cluster of symbols flickered on to one of the many screens that littered the surface and there was a low electronic burbling from somewhere deep in the machinery below him.

Rose twisted in her sleep again, her brow furrowing. The Doctor's gaze went from the console to Rose and back again, and he pulled off his glasses, chewing on one of the arms thoughtfully.

'Now what are you two talking about? All girls together, is it?'

Pushing his glasses back into his pocket, the Doctor leaned forward and started tapping at the controls.

Rose knew she was dreaming. She knew because she could see herself, as if she was another person, from just over her right shoulder. It was odd, looking at the back of your own head, seeing everything from someone else's perspective. A small part of her subconscious was aware of the fact that her hair was getting straggly and needed a cut, perhaps a bit of colour, but mostly she noticed that she was outdoors, in the rain and floating a couple of metres off the ground.

She looked around, taking in the vague, unreal surroundings of her dream. As dreams went, it wasn't particularly exotic. She was on the coast, almost certainly Britain. The scrubby grass and tangle of gorse bushes were unmistakably British. And yes, there were sheep grazing in the distant fields. As far as she was aware, sheep were peculiar to Earth; in her travels with the Doctor she hadn't yet come across any space sheep...

She giggled, aware that it was turning out to be a very odd and mundane dream, when she noticed the child looking at her: a small child in pyjamas, clutching a soft toy, staring straight at her and smiling. For some reason that she couldn't explain, a shiver ran down Rose's spine.

The child started to laugh and the sky darkened, lightning cracking through the air.

Rose found herself moving now, swooping over the gorse, sailing out off the cliff and sweeping down over the water. Dark shapes loomed up from the darkness: cliffs, jagged rocks, a lighthouse, its paintwork faded and peeling, the glass in the lamp room cracked and broken.

Pale, sickly green light washed over her and she was aware of masked figures watching her, chattering in a strange incomprehensible language. The lighthouse sped past and a roar suddenly cut through the air, harsh and terrifying.

Rose's dream rapidly degenerated into nightmare as a vile four-armed creature hauled itself from the sea below her. Steam curled around it and the sea boiled as it lumbered up on to dry land, rain hissing on its armoured skin. Its claws reached out for something lying on the ground and Rose realised with horror that it was a young man, fishing equipment scattered around him, his arms raised in a futile attempt to ward the creature off as he scrabbled backwards over the wet grass.

Rose desperately wanted to look away, already knowing what was going to come next, but, as is the way with nightmares, she couldn't tear her eyes from the horror unfolding before her.

The creature let out another guttural bellow. Flames leapt from its throat and Rose felt a wave of hot, fetid air wash over her. A monstrous arm swung into the air and she gasped as she caught sight of wickedly barbed claws glinting in the rain. As the arm came down, the young fisherman slumped backwards, his blood staining the rocks.

The creature turned and fixed Rose with blazing eyes. It roared again, reaching out for her. Rose tried to scream, but no sound would come from her throat. Above the roars of the creature she thought she could hear the sound of a child laughing. Then the huge taloned hands closed around her...

And she woke with a start, almost tumbling from the chair.

The Doctor looked up from a screen, concern in his eyes.

'Are you all right?'

Rose ran a hand through her hair, her eyes flicking around the shadows that pooled in the corners of the console room.

'Yeah, a dream, that's all. A nightmare.' She shivered, pulling the Doctor's coat around her shoulders.'

'Not surprising really, is it? Considering the stuff we end up seeing…'

She rubbed sleep from her eyes and shuffled over to where the Doctor was prodding at the console. 'Don't you *ever* sleep?'

'Nah. Tried it once, didn't like it. I prefer it when it's quiet.'

Rose gave a snort. 'Yeah, right. Like it's *ever* quiet with you.' She nodded at the console. 'What are you doing?'

'It seems that you're not the only one who was having nightmares.' He cocked his head to one side and peered at her. 'Can you remember what your dream was about?'

'Things. Creatures…'

'Creatures?'

'Yeah, I was at the coast. Not a beach with sand, but lots of rocks… and a lighthouse. There was a storm. And a kid, a little boy who kept laughing. Then this thing came out of the sea, a big sea monster sort of thing, four arms, breathing fire. It killed a man, a fisherman, and it was starting to turn on me…'

The Doctor's frown deepened. 'Well, isn't that strange.'

Rose was puzzled. 'Why? What's up with that? It was just a dream, wasn't it?'

The Doctor nodded at the screen in front of him. 'Seems like you and the TARDIS both had the same dream. We picked up some very odd readings while you were asleep. I've been tracing them back to their source.'

Rose crossed to his side, peering over his shoulder. 'Oh, my God!'

On the screen was a long stretch of rocky coast, harsh and windswept. Out in the waves was a jagged lump of black rock, the long, slender shape of a lighthouse stabbing towards the heavy clouds.

'That's the place!' Rose stared in disbelief. 'That's where I was in my dream!'

The Doctor looked up at her with a mysterious twinkle in his eyes. 'And if the place is real, then the creature might be real as well. Shall we go and take a look?'

Before Rose had a chance to answer the Doctor darted round the console, spinning wheels and pumping energetically at some of the TARDIS's more jerry-rigged controls.

With a grind of ancient engines, the TARDIS started to turn, and Rose realised with a thrill of terror that quite possibly she was about to confront the creature from her nightmare.

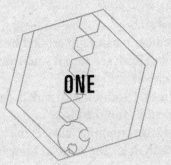

ONE

The moon gleamed fitfully through the long fingers of cloud that scudded across its face, sending sparkling highlights flickering over the foaming waves. The storm that had whipped the ocean into such a frenzy was far away now, the rumble of thunder just a distant boom over the hills, the lightning a faint glow occasionally illuminating the sky.

A new sound joined the rhythmic hiss of waves on shingle, a rasping, grinding noise, rising and falling in pitch, building in volume until, with a loud thump, the TARDIS appeared from nowhere on the cliff top, incongruous among the windswept gorse.

With a rattling of the latch, the door swung inwards and the Doctor stepped out into the cold night air, coat billowing in the wind. Rose emerged tentatively after him, looking around nervously.

The Doctor spread his arms wide and took a long, deep breath. 'Come on, Rose. Get a good lungful of that fresh sea air.'

Rose pulled her parka tight around her. 'You'll get a great lungful of fresh sea *water* if you're not careful. It's freezing out here!'

'It's a bit fresh, I'll admit.' He twirled, fixing her with a piercing gaze. 'Is this the place?'

Rose nodded, stepping closer to his side and shivering. 'Yeah. It is. The same as I saw in my dream. It's weird.'

'Marvellous!' The Doctor smiled happily, pulling the TARDIS key from his pocket and locking the police box door.

Rose turned slowly around. Everything was horribly familiar. The tall, jagged cliffs, the brooding sky. Along the coast she could see the lights from the village, tucked into the curve of the bay, a tiny harbour jutting out into the cold grey sea.

A noise made her jump, a long wail, drawn out and plaintive. On the next headland over she could see the lights of a lonely farmhouse, a trail of smoke whipped from its chimney by the driving wind.

She caught the Doctor by the arm. 'Listen.'

The Doctor turned from the TARDIS, head cocked to one side. The sound came again, high-pitched and almost cat-like, cutting through the sound of the wind.

Rose felt goosebumps run down her spine. 'It's a baby. Poor thing sounds terrified.'

'It's not happy, certainly.' The Doctor pulled a pair of opera glasses from his coat and peered at the lights blazing from the distant farm buildings. 'And keeping the house awake by the look of things.'

'Where are we exactly?' Rose asked.

'Wales, according to the instruments.' The Doctor swung his gaze out towards the horizon. 'West coast, just along from Tenby, I think. Village called Ynys Du.'

'Come again?'

'Black Island. Not the kind of place you usually find ravening four-armed creatures, I must admit, but probably very good for sea bass. Ah…'

'What is it?'

The Doctor nodded out to sea. 'Your mysterious lighthouse?'

Rose followed his gaze. The racing clouds cleared from the moon for a moment and she could make out the tall, slender shape rising from the jagged mound of black rock in the bay. She shivered again, though this time not from the cold.

'Yeah. That's it.'

The Doctor adjusted a small dial on the opera glasses, peering intently at the lighthouse through the computer-enhanced lenses. 'Doesn't look as though it's been used for years. Shame. Make a nice little home, that would. Tricky to get your milk delivered, but no problem with the neighbours.'

'Great if you like fish.'

'Exactly!' He lowered the glasses and turned to her. 'Where did you see the fisherman?'

Rose nodded down the cliff. A well-worn path snaked through the gorse, winding its way to an untidy jumble of rocks at the water's edge.

'Down there, on the rocks.'

The Doctor raised his opera glasses again, scanning the coast. 'No sign of any monsters… Hello…'

Rose's heart jumped. 'What is it? Have you seen it?'

'I think there's someone there.' The Doctor frowned. 'Thought I caught a glimpse of someone at the shoreline.'

'The creature?'

'Not unless it's taken to wearing a long white coat.' He tucked the glasses back into his pocket. 'Come on. Let's take a closer look.'

The Doctor set off down the rocky path, his own coat billowing out behind him.

'Hang about!'

Rose set off after him a little more cautiously. The rain and spray had made the path treacherous and gorse barbs tore at her clothes as she pushed her way down the narrow sheep track. By the time she reached the bottom, the hems of her jeans were streaked with mud, her trainers sodden.

The path ended at a narrow spit of land, scrubby grass that sloped down to the sea. Huge wet boulders, flecked with foam and seaweed lay jumbled up against the shore. The Doctor was squatted on top of one of them, seemingly oblivious to the spray that swirled around him each time a wave crashed in. He was prodding at the rock with his sonic screwdriver.

He glanced up at her as she picked her way over. 'Nothing. No sign of monster, fisherman, anything…'

'What about your white-coated figure?'

'No.' The Doctor pursed his lips. 'No sign of him, or her, either.'

'Well, they can't have got past us. There's no other way down from the cliffs and they'd be mad to take a boat out in this. You must have been seeing things.'

The Doctor hopped down from his rock. 'Perhaps I dreamt them.'

'That's not funny.'

'Neither is this. Look.'

The Doctor pointed at a rock pool, little more than a crevice in the wet rock. Rose raised a hand to her mouth. Among the seaweed and barnacles the pool was bright red.

The Doctor knelt down, scanning the liquid with his screwdriver. Rose knelt next to him.

'Is it…'

'Blood, yes.' The Doctor's face was grim. 'There's more here. And here.'

Leading Rose by the hand, the Doctor followed the gruesome trail across the rocks, pool after pool filled with diluted blood.

Their route led back from the rocks to a patch of flattened grass. The Doctor knelt down once more and pressed his palm to the ground. It came away stained a deep red. Rose stared in horror at the large dark patch that discoloured the grass.

'There's so much of it.'

The Doctor's face was grim. 'So where's the body?'

'Perhaps the thing took it back into the sea. You know. Food?'

'Possibly.'

Rose looked around. 'No, hang about. He was a fisherman. He had bags, rods and stuff. They've gone too.'

'Well, I can't see our mysterious creature being an avid fishing fan somehow.' The Doctor shook his head and wiped his hands on a patch of clean grass. 'No. Someone has been here, cleaning up after their pet.'

Rose looked at him in horror. 'You don't think –'

'I'm not sure what to think yet.' He gave her a reassuring smile. 'But we're not going to find out anything more down here, not tonight at any rate. We should try the village. Ask around. Someone must know something.'

'We're gonna have to try and find his friends. His family. Let them know that he's…'

'That could raise some awkward questions. But yes, you're right. We'll have to do it.' The Doctor caught her by the hand. 'C'mon. Let's get away from here.'

And with that the two of them started to pick their way back up the slippery path to the cliff top, Rose leading the way, pushing determinedly through the gorse, trying to avoid the signs of violence that were now so obvious all around them.

Something made the Doctor glance back at the dark shape of the lighthouse in the bay. A glint of light caught his eye. He stopped, fumbling for the opera glasses in his pocket again, but whatever the light was it vanished just as suddenly as it had appeared.

He frowned, unsure of what he had seen.

'What is it?'

Rose had stopped on the path ahead of him, looking back in concern.

'Nothing. C'mon. We're nearly at the top.'

Rose shrugged and started upwards again, and after a few seconds the Doctor followed. There was something dangerous here, of that he was certain, and in retrospect wandering around wet cliff tops in the dark in pursuit of a vicious monster wasn't the most sensible decision he had ever made. The village was the obvious place to go. Lights and people, and perhaps some answers.

He clambered the last few steps to the top of the cliff. Rose was waiting for him, the hood of her parka pulled tight against the wind. Fat drops of rain were starting to whip in from the sea again and a clap of thunder sounded, closer now as the storm circled around for a second time.

'Now where?' Rose shouted above the wind.

The Doctor spun on his heel. A clear track led away from the cliffs towards a patch of woodland that arced down towards the village in the bay. A coastal path. Probably heaving with walkers and families when the weather was good.

'This way!'

They raced for the cover of the wood as the storm finally broke again and the wind swirled icy rain around them. They reached the tree line breathless, the Doctor's hair plastered to his forehead.

Rose giggled at him. 'Why can't you ever take us somewhere nice and warm?'

'Hey!' The Doctor looked indignant. 'I took you to New Earth! Apple grass, remember?'

'Yeah! Not exactly a relaxing break, though, being taken over...'

'The sign of a good holiday!' He flicked the water from his fringe. 'Anyway, now I've brought you to a nice wood. A nice *wet* wood.'

'A nice wet, dark wood.'

'Yes.' The Doctor peered into the gloom. 'Actually it's more *tulgy* than wet. Yes. Definitely a tulgy wood.' He set off down the leaf-strewn path. 'Lovely word "tulgy". Doesn't get enough use. Very good for describing woods... And puddings. I've had some wonderfully tulgy puddings in my time.'

Rose hurried to catch him up. 'Tulgy puddings? What sort of restaurants have you been eating in?'

'You've never had a tulgy pudding? Oh, you haven't lived.'

Rose hooked her arm through his. 'OK, you can buy me a tulgy pudding some day.'

The Doctor smiled at her, aware that she needed her mind taking off what she had seen on the rocks.

'Done.' The two of them set off along the path. 'Lewis Carroll. He was an odd one. Real name was Charles Lutwidge Dodgson. Completely denied having anything to do with the Alice books. Daft as a brush. You'd have liked him! Loved inventing words. Ever read *Jabberwocky*? Loads of good words in there. "Tulgy", "whiffling", "galumphing". And "burbled". How come "burbled" gets to be in the *Oxford English Dictionary* but "tulgy" doesn't? Hm?'

Before Rose could reply a low rumbling growl brought the two of them to a sudden halt.

'That wasn't a burble,' she whispered.

'No.'

The Doctor's eyes darted from tree to tree. The wood was a jumble of long shadows and tangled undergrowth. The moon cast pale pools of light among the wet leaves as the clouds uncovered it for a moment, then the trees were plunged into darkness once again.

The Doctor rummaged in his pocket and there was the harsh rasp of a match on sandpaper. Light flared, casting flickering shadows through the dripping wood.

Rose grasped the proffered match gratefully as the Doctor lit another.

'Everlasting matches?' she asked.

The Doctor nodded, eyes narrowing as he desperately searched for the source of the growl.

There was a crackle of twigs and leaves as something large and unseen slowly circled them.

'I don't suppose you've got a vorpal blade tucked away in that coat of yours?'

The Doctor gave her a brief smile. 'Only a vorpal penknife, I'm afraid. And a blunt one at that.'

There was another throaty rumble and Rose clutched the Doctor's arm.

'Over there!'

The Doctor followed her gaze. A large shape crouched in the shadows of an oak tree, the light from the flickering matches gleaming in its eyes. The Doctor could count at least fourteen eyes. He reached out for Rose.

'Rose, I want you to take my hand and start backing away slowly. Don't run until I say "Run."'

The two of them started backing away from the shadowed monster. With a shattering roar, it broke cover, crashing through the wet leaves towards them.

'Freeze!' the Doctor hissed.

The creature was huge and grey, its face a mass of shiny black eyes and jutting fangs, the body slick with vile-smelling slime. Eight thick, fleshy tentacles sprang from the glistening body, writhing through the mulch of the woodland floor, dragging the creature forward. Dozens of huge suckers pulsed wetly on each tentacle.

The Doctor peered at it in puzzled fascination. The creature seemed... wrong, somehow, thrown together, not the product of any normal evolutionary process. He took a step forward, intending to get a closer look, but Rose hauled him back frantically.

'What are you doing?'

'Wanted to see if I could get a better look at it, have a bit of a chat, find out what it's doing here.' He gave her a stern look. 'It's not at all like you described it. Nothing like! Wrong number of arms for starters. We'll have to give you a few lessons in alien identification when we get back to the TARDIS.'

'*If* we get back to the TARDIS, you mean. In case you hadn't noticed, that thing is looking at us as if we're lunch. Besides, it's not the wrong number of arms because that's not the thing I saw.'

There was a shattering roar from behind them. The two of them spun to see another creature emerging from the shadows.

'*That's* the one I saw,' said Rose.

'Oh. Right-o. Sorry.' The Doctor gave her a weak smile. 'I think it might be time to run now.'

Rose rolled her eyes. 'You think?'

'Run!'

The Doctor and Rose plunged off the path, pushing through the tangle of tree roots and brambles. Branches whipped at their faces, catching on their clothes. Behind them they could hear the frustrated roars of the creatures and the sound of trees crashing to the floor as the two monsters tried to tear their way through in pursuit.

'They're too big to follow us in here!' shouted the Doctor. 'Keep to where the wood is dense!'

The two of them struggled forward, ducking under fallen trees, scrambling up muddy banks. Finally they stumbled into a small clearing and the Doctor waved at Rose to stop.

'Slow down. I think we've lost them.'

Rose slumped against a tree, breathing hard. She tilted her head back, letting raindrops from the leaves splash on to her face.

'I'll tell you one thing. Being with you keeps a girl fit.'

The Doctor beamed breathlessly at her. 'Fun to be with *and* good for you. Gotta be just what the doctor ordered.'

'What were those things?'

'Dunno. Nothing I've ever seen before.'

'Something you don't know… I knew there had to be something.'

'It happens occasionally. Tell you what I do know, though…'

'Yeah?'

'We're nearly out of the woods.'

He nodded through the trees. Ahead of them, about 200 metres away, yellow light glowed warmly.

'Street lamps?'

The Doctor nodded.

'Civilisation, of a sort.'

Rose smiled, then froze. The rain splashing on to her face had suddenly got warm. And thick.

She wiped a hand across her face and saw strands of sticky slime trailing from her fingers. She looked up in disgust. And screamed.

A huge centipede loomed over her, hanging from an overhead branch. It must have been over two metres long, its thick body bristling with hairs and thick slime dripping from razor-sharp mandibles. It lunged at her, hissing viciously.

Rose stumbled backwards, her foot slipping on the wet earth. She crashed to the ground, the air punched out of her. The centipede gave a hiss of triumph and surged forward.

Suddenly there was a sharp piercing whine and the creature dropped from the tree, writhing on the ground in agony, mandibles snapping uselessly at the air. The Doctor stood on the other side of the clearing, sonic screwdriver held out before him, the blue light at its lip gleaming brightly in the gloom.

He darted forward, dodging out of the way of the squirming monster, and hauled Rose to her feet. He handed her a large spotted handkerchief and she wiped her face gratefully.

'How many more of these things are there?'

The Doctor nodded over her shoulder, his face grim. 'Lots, unfortunately.'

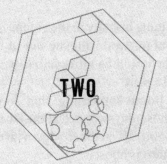

TWO

The Doctor and Rose hared through the wood, desperate to reach the distant lights. Through the trees behind them came monsters of every description: big ones, small ones, all colours and shapes. Some bounded forward on muscular legs, others skittered from tree to tree. They slithered, they crawled, some even flew, pursuing them through the dark, baying like a pack of hounds. The noise was deafening.

Rose's breath was burning in her chest. She fought the instinct to look back. She felt that any minute now one of the monstrosities behind them would reach out with a feeler or claw and snatch her into the middle of the howling throng. She remembered the blood pools on the beach, dark stains all that was left of a young man, and started to run faster.

The lights ahead of them were tantalisingly close, but Rose just wasn't sure what happened once they reached them. She glanced at the Doctor, who was racing alongside her. His eyes were fixed on the lights at the edge of the wood, his jaw was set. Suddenly she knew that it would be all right. He was the Doctor. And he had a plan!

At that point something that looked like an oversized mosquito swooped at the Doctor's head, its wings droning. It stabbed down at him with a wickedly sharp proboscis.

The Doctor batted it away frantically and as it darted off, buzzing angrily, its long legs brushed Rose's hair. She jerked backwards, stumbling and almost falling.

The Doctor caught her and hauled her to her feet. 'Come on! We're almost there!'

They burst from the woods on to a tarmacked road, a cul-de-sac, lined with parked cars and small identical houses. Street lamps cast a harsh yellow glow and down the hill Rose could see the lights of the harbour.

She hurled herself into the middle of the road, spinning round to stare back at the wood, oblivious to the rain. The creatures hovered at the tree line, as if wary about stepping out into the light. One of them, a squat lizard with claws that dragged along the floor, edged forward tentatively. Rose glanced nervously over at the Doctor. He was staring around at the houses in disbelief.

'No, no, no. This is all wrong!'

'What is it?' Rose's heart was in her mouth. 'What's the matter?'

'This estate!' The Doctor nodded at the houses. 'It's all wrong. Not in keeping with the rest of the village at all! Why do they let people build things like this? It's not on, you know, modern estate like this in a conservation area. I've a good mind to write to the council.'

Rose was speechless. The monsters were emerging from the trees now, there was nowhere to hide and the Doctor was wittering on about sympathetic building styles!

'Still,' he went on, 'it's probably attracting new people to the area and everyone living round here's obviously doing quite well. Couple of cars in each driveway, quite a few four-by-fours... Which is good, 'cause it allows me to do this!'

He raised his sonic screwdriver, winked at Rose and pressed his thumb against the button.

Every car alarm went off simultaneously. Rose clamped her hands over her ears, trying to drown out the cacophony. The noise was horrendous, but she thought she could just make out the howls of the creatures over the din.

Then, just as suddenly, it stopped.

Rose looked up. The Doctor was standing in the middle of the street, grinning happily. He tucked his sonic screwdriver back into his pocket and nodded over at her.

'That worked, then.'

The monsters were gone. It was as if they had never existed. She and the Doctor were in what looked like an ordinary housing estate. Unremarkable. Boring.

Lights started to come on and curtains were pulled back as people stared out into their driveways. A door opened and a man in his dressing gown peered out at them, his face uncertain, angry.

Rose cocked her head to one side, listening. From inside the house she could hear a child crying.

Rose looked over at the Doctor. 'Listen.'

The Doctor had heard it too.

'Yes.'

The man in the dressing gown took a tentative step towards them. 'What are you doing out there?' he shouted. 'Don't you realise how late it is?'

More lights were coming on all over the estate now, more curtains twitching. The Doctor started to make his way down the hill towards the harbour. He turned to Rose.

'Come on. We'd better make ourselves scarce. Probably not a good idea to stay outside.'

Rose hurried to catch him up. 'You think those things are still going to be around? I thought you'd got rid of them.'

'The noise seemed to scare them off, but I've got no idea where they went. And I certainly don't know where they came from.'

* * *

The faceless modern style of the estate gave way to a more rustic flavour, with small stone cottages, shops full of postcards and tourist paraphernalia, tearooms with posters advertising trips around the bay in their windows. Fishing boats and small yachts bobbed in the harbour, halyards clanking in the wind.

The Doctor strode down to the harbour wall, hands thrust into the pockets of his coat, and stared out across the water.

'That's one bit of the puzzle, out there. Sure of it.'

Rose followed his gaze. 'The lighthouse?'

'Yeah. Maybe. Thought I caught a glimpse of a light out there when we were up on the cliff top, just before we went into the woods.'

'And that's what's causing the creatures?'

'Could be. Need to get out there and have a gander at some point.'

Rose peered over the wall at the churning water. 'Bit cold for a dip.'

'I was thinking a nice little boat trip.'

'You can't just nick someone's boat!'

'I wasn't going to!' The Doctor looked indignant. 'I was going to use my boyish charm to persuade one of the locals to take me out there.'

'Oh yeah?' Rose stifled a smile. 'And where were you hoping to try out this "boyish charm" of yours. In case you haven't noticed, it's the middle of the night and the place is deserted.'

The Doctor turned and nodded at the large, imposing building that dominated the seafront.

'The pub.'

'Bit late for that, isn't it?'

'Lights are still on. Perhaps they're having a lock-in. Come on.'

Beth Hardy was changing over the bottle of single malt, trying to ignore the noises that floated on the wind outside. The spirits had been going down fast since… since it all started. She'd have to get another order in with the wholesalers, make up another excuse about why her order had almost doubled in the last month. Not that they were complaining about it, of course. The Red Lion had become their favourite client of late.

The public bar was full as usual, but there was none of the usual chatter that you'd associate with a busy pub. Groups of people sat hunched over their pints and glasses, silent and grim-faced, occasionally looking up if some distant noise reached them from outside.

Upstairs she could hear the sobs of her daughter, Ali, and the deep rich tones of her husband, soothing her, calming her. It was the same every evening as Ali's bedtime approached, the false bravado that came as night started to fall, then the anger that there was nothing that her parents could do, and finally the tears as sleep slowly started to take a hold of her.

Beth could see the pain in the faces of a dozen men at the bar, knowing that they, like her, had reached a point where they just didn't know what to do any more and had found other ways of shutting the heartache out.

From the other side of the bar, in the restaurant area, came the sound of raised voices: accusations and counter-accusations. She could hear Bob Perry, the harbour master, followed by the dulcet tones of Reverend Hall appealing for calm. Beth shook her head. Nothing good ever came of these village meetings. Old arguments reared their head time after time, the parents like herself desperately looking for answers and the vicar repeating that they should have faith. Beth's own faith was at breaking point.

The door behind her opened and Mervyn, her husband, stepped back into the bar, giving her a weak smile.

'She says she's going to read for a while. That new *Invisible Detective* book Maureen gave her.'

Beth nodded. They both knew that it was just delaying the inevitable. However much Ali fought against it, sleep always won the battle and the nightmares would start again.

'How's it going through there?'

Beth shrugged. 'Just the usual. Bob and the vicar sniping at each other, one blaming the Devil, the other blaming anything and everything.'

'I'll go and see if I can calm things down a little.'

He squeezed her arm and crossed the room. Beth sighed and picked up the bottle of whisky from the bar. She was lifting it up to the waiting optic when the door swung open with a flurry of wind.

The bottle nearly slipped from her fingers, thumping against the side of the bar. In the doorway stood a tall, thin-faced man in a long brown coat and a young girl huddled into a parka.

Everyone in the pub turned to look at the Doctor and Rose, surprise etched on their faces. Seemingly oblivious to the attention he was attracting, the Doctor strode across to the bar, a friendly smile on his face. Rose followed him nervously, aware of the stares. The babble of conversation from the restaurant had stopped too and the pub became frighteningly quiet.

'Right, Rose. What are you having? They've got those little cheesy biscuits! I love them!'

Rose tugged at the sleeve of his coat. 'Doctor, I really don't think these people are happy to see us.'

Beth felt her heart jump. 'Doctor? You're a Doctor?'

'Yes.' The man gave her a puzzled look. 'Why? Is there something wrong here?'

'Yes. Please…'

'That's enough, Beth!' Mervyn's voice boomed across the bar. He pushed his way through the tangle of tables. 'Who are you? How did you get here?'

The Doctor turned to face him. 'I'm the Doctor, this is Rose. We walked.'

'Walked?'

There was a low murmur from the watching regulars.

'Yes. Through the woods. Quite an interesting walk, wouldn't you say, Rose? Lots of wildlife.'

Mervyn flinched. 'I don't know what you mean.'

'And we found a large pool of blood by the shore.' The Doctor's voice was hard now. 'I don't suppose you'd know anything about that either?'

Beth saw her husband's fists clench.

'I think that you'd better go.'

Beth clutched at her husband's arm. 'Mervyn! We can't send them back out again. Not at night. You know we can't! He says he's a doctor. He might be able to help! What harm can it do?'

'Mummy, what's going on?'

The tired voice cut through the bar. Beth turned to see her daughter standing in the doorway, rubbing her eyes, a colouring book tucked under her arm. 'I heard the door open. I thought you said no one could go outside.'

Beth scooped Ali up into her arms. 'That's right, baby. It's dangerous outside.'

'I've been drawing. Drawing the monsters.'

She held out her book. There was a crude pencil

drawing of a tall grey monster with four arms and huge teeth. Beth heard the girl Rose gasp.

'Doctor, that's the thing we just saw in the woods. The thing from my dream!'

The Doctor plucked the drawing book from Ali's hand, studied it for a moment, then fixed Beth with a piercing stare. 'What *is* going on here?'

Rose sat close to the roaring fire in the corner of the pub, sipping gratefully at a mug of hot chocolate. The Doctor was at the bar, talking animatedly with a gaggle of villagers. The arrival of the little girl, Ali, couldn't have been better-timed. Rose was sure there would have been a fight if she hadn't turned up when she did, and the Doctor didn't look like he was the brawling type.

The Doctor's psychic paper had helped as well, of course. Mervyn, the landlord, had asked to see some identification and the Doctor had been only too happy to oblige. Whatever it was that the villagers saw on the paper, their relief was obvious and their hostility quickly evaporated. Now they were only too eager to accept the Doctor's offer of help.

Ali pushed another sheet of paper in front of Rose. The little girl seemed to have taken an instant liking to her and was now perched on a barstool on the opposite side of the table, colouring furiously in her book.

Rose picked up the drawing. Another monster, all fangs and horns and fur. Whatever was going on here was clearly terrifying the children.

A flurry of rain rattled the window and Ali looked up, fearful.

Rose patted her hand. 'It's just the wind.'

Ali nodded and returned to her drawing, but she kept a wary eye on the curtains.

At the bar the Doctor was getting frustrated.

'But surely you've tried to tell someone about what's going on?'

'Oh yes, sure.' Bob Perry took a long gulp of his pint. 'Monsters roaming the streets, that's really going to sound good. Think that the Assembly in Cardiff has got a department that deals with that, do you?'

'You might be surprised...'

'The phones go dead.' Beth's voice was timid. 'As soon as they appear, nothing but static.'

The Doctor gave her a curious look, leaned across the bar and picked up the phone that stood next to the till. There was no dialling tone, just an undulating hiss.

He frowned. 'Every time the creatures appear?'

Beth nodded.

'OK, so you can't phone. But you can prove these things exist, surely? Just get the authorities to come here after dark!'

'And go roaming through the woods with a torch? You've seen what it's like out there.'

'If we stay indoors they don't bother us.' Beth wouldn't meet his gaze. 'And the days are safe.'

The Doctor looked at her. 'Safe? We… saw a young man, a fisherman out on the cliff tops. And now there are just pools of blood. What about him?'

The villagers shuffled uncomfortably, staring into their glasses.

'Dead?' Bob's voice was shaky. 'They've never killed anything before…'

'Well, they have now.' The Doctor's voice was firm. 'Who was he?'

'Tourist. Camping out on the headland, I thought.'

'If he was out after dark…' Beth's voice tailed off.

'And none of you bothered to warn him?'

The villagers looked sheepishly away from the Doctor and for a while no one spoke. Then Mervyn shook his head and said, 'You must be wrong. He's probably just gone home. Saw how the weather had changed and went home.'

There was a general mutter of agreement.

The Doctor was incredulous. 'You can't just ignore this as if it never happened!'

'They've never killed anything. You've no proof. No proof at all!'

'There was blood on the rocks!'

'We've only got your word for that.'

The Doctor shook his head. For whatever reason, the villagers were refusing to accept the reality of the situation. This was more than just pig-headedness. There was genuine confusion in their faces. It was as if they were finding any excuse they could, anything to avoid confronting the problem head on.

'His fault, isn't it?' A broad Welsh accent cut across the pub. 'He came back! I told him not to come back!'

The villagers groaned and there were angry mutterings.

'Shut up, Bronwyn!' someone shouted. 'No one asked you!'

'No one ever does, but it doesn't mean I'm wrong.'

A stout lady in her seventies pushed her way to the bar and stood there, tapping on the polished surface with a bony finger. Her silver hair still had streaks of auburn and her eyes were a brilliant grey.

'All started as soon as Nathaniel came back.'

'Give it up, Bronwyn.'

The pub erupted into a babble of raised voices. This was obviously an old argument.

'Who's Nathaniel?' The Doctor had to shout above the hubbub. 'Who is he?'

'Nathaniel Morton, a retired industrialist,' said Mervyn. 'Took over the old rectory at the beginning of the year. Spent a fortune on the place, putting new windows in, new roof.'

'Thinks he's lord of the manor,' Bronwyn sneered.

The Doctor shrugged. 'And?'

'He's a local boy, or was, a long time ago.'

'Local? Hah!' Bronwyn snorted contemptuously. 'Turned his back on us, he did. Betrayed us. Came back when he said he never would.'

Mervyn turned on her. 'You've been warned, Bronwyn Ceredig. We're not interested in your feud with Morton. Now keep quiet or you're barred.'

Bronwyn shot him a filthy look and shuffled back over to her seat by the window. The Doctor watched her thoughtfully.

'Not a close family friend, then.'

'Ah, take no notice of her, Doctor. She's a mad old woman. Had some problem with Morton when they were younger.'

'And she doesn't approve of him setting up shop in the rectory?'

'He's turned the place into some kind of private nursing home. Don't know much about it. He never comes into town. Sends his people out to do all his shopping, keeps himself to himself.'

'And the creatures started appearing once he'd arrived?'

Mervyn shook his head. 'Ah, she seems to think so. Can't see how, unless he's breeding them up there. He's just a harmless old man.'

'Harmless?' Bronwyn's voice rang out again. 'You're fools if you can't see it!'

'Enough!' Mervyn slammed his fist down on the bar. 'I warned you.'

People had started to murmur angrily once again. Bronwyn got to her feet.

'All right, Mervyn Hardy. I know when I'm not wanted.' She started to struggle into her coat. 'Don't know why I bother.'

Beth hurried over to her. 'You can't go out alone, Bronwyn. Not with them out there. Come on. I'll get you another drink.'

The Doctor watched as Beth led the old woman back to her seat. It seemed that there was more going on in Ynys Du than he had first realised.

He turned back to Mervyn. 'What about the lighthouse in the bay? Is that inhabited?'

Mervyn shook his head. 'Been derelict for years. Why?'

'Just curious. Thought I saw something out there. It's probably nothing.' The Doctor shot Rose a glance. 'Tomorrow I'll make a proper investigation. We'll sort this. I promise.'

The meeting started to break up. Huddling together for safety, groups headed nervously out into the night, racing to the safety of cars and nearby houses. No one was prepared to walk far or alone. Even Bronwyn was escorted to a car by one of the locals.

Beth squeezed the Doctor's hand. 'Thank you.'

He gave her a reassuring smile and crossed the room to where Rose was sitting, dropping on to a stool and giving Ali a cheeky grin.

The little girl was now starting to slump over her drawing book and her her eyes were flickering shut. She gave a huge yawn.

'Oh, don't start that!' said the Doctor. 'You'll set me off!'

He gave a mock yawn, stretching theatrically in his seat. Ali regarded him suspiciously.

'Come on, young lady.' Beth came over and tousled her daughter's hair.

Ali's smile faded. 'Do I have to?'

Beth nodded. 'But I'll read to you for a while if you like.'

'Sounds like a good deal to me.' The Doctor leaned forward, his eyes twinkling. 'A nice story. No monsters. *Moxx in Socks* was always my favourite! "Moxx! Moxx in socks! Moxx in socks with Phlox!"'

Rose rolled her eyes in despair and Ali giggled.

'You're silly,' the little girl said.

The Doctor nodded. 'Yes, I probably am.'

Beth hoisted her daughter into her arms, carrying her across the bar. At the door she stopped and turned back.

'Doctor…'

The Doctor looked up. There was fear in Beth's face.

'Ali is all we've got…' Her voice trembled. 'I don't want to lose her.'

The Doctor frowned. 'What makes you think that you're going to lose her?'

'It's just… These things, these monsters, that boy who died…'

The front door banged as Mervyn stepped back in from the car park, slamming home the bolts, glaring at his wife.

Beth shook her head. 'It's nothing. You'll stay here tonight?'

The Doctor smiled at her. 'Thank you. I wasn't looking forward to a trek back through the woods.'

'I'll get Mervyn to make up the guest rooms in the attic for you.'

'Oh, don't worry about me.' The Doctor waved a hand. 'I've got some thinking to do. But if you could sort out a bed for Rose.'

'All right. If you're sure. Goodnight, Doctor.' She smiled at Rose. 'Mervyn will have your room ready in a few minutes. And thank you again, both of you.'

The Doctor watched, puzzled, as Beth and her husband vanished up the stairs.

Rose leaned forward, whispering conspiratorially. 'What was all that about?'

'Not sure.' The Doctor pursed his lips, then picked up some of the drawings Ali had left on the table.

'Beth's not telling us something,' Rose continued.

The Doctor perched his glasses on the end of his nose and peered at the drawings. 'Yes, you're right, but we're not going to find out anything more tonight.'

'So what's going on here, eh? And what's with the

old biddy? She's definitely got the hump about something… You think that she's right, that it's something to do with this bloke at the rectory?'

'Bronwyn's another lady with secrets, that's for certain. But retired industrialists breeding creatures and letting them loose in the woods? Doesn't feel right to me.'

'It's spooked the kids here, though,' said Rose. 'They're terrified.'

'I'm not surprised with things like this roaming through the local woods!'

As if on cue, there was a guttural roar from outside.

The Doctor dropped the drawings back on to the table with a deep sigh. 'I think we should pay a visit to Nathaniel Morton at the rectory and then get out to the lighthouse. But we're not going to be able to do much in the dark if those creatures are still active, so I'm afraid we're going to have to wait until morning. You'd better get up to bed.'

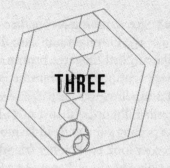

THREE

The morning sun came up bright and harsh over the sea, sending tendrils of mist spiralling into the air from the wet bracken. Ali crept through the damp undergrowth, keeping to the shadows of the rectory's long stone perimeter wall. The house itself loomed ahead of her, vast and imposing, wet slates glinting in the morning light, the windows dark and ominous.

She looked back at the gateway, where a cluster of expectant faces were watching her. She could hear Billy Palmer urging her on.

'Go on! Just do it!' he hissed. 'Hiding in the shadows is no good!'

Ali turned back towards the house. The wall surrounded an untidy garden that was bordered with gravel paths. Rhododendron bushes that had been allowed to grow wild towered over walls and stragglylooking shrubs fought their way through the brambles in the flowerbeds.

She broke cover, sprinting across the wet grass, not wanting to use the gravel path in case the noise gave her away. She reached the large broken birdbath that stood in front of the house and hunched down behind it, her heart pounding.

The door was right opposite her now. The big black door with its peeling paint and old-fashioned knocker. Ali took another look back at her friends. They were all urging her on. She closed her eyes, trying to control her fear. All of them had done this. She was the only one left. She had to do it.

She *wanted* to do it.

Taking a deep breath, she darted across the lawn crouched low, not daring to look up at those horrible black windows in case a face appeared in one of them. She ducked into the porch, grabbing the big brass knocker and letting it crash back against the door. Once. Twice. Three times. She could hear the noise echoing around the hallway of the damp old house.

Giddy with excitement, Ali whirled and hared back across the lawn to her waiting friends. She'd done it! She'd done it! She was part of the gang. When she reached the gate, most of that gang were already running, laughing and shoving at each other.

Billy Palmer had waited for her and was now grinning like a loon.

'Didn't think you were gonna do it!'

'It was easy,' lied Ali.

Giggling, the two of them ran to catch up with their mates.

Nathaniel Morton watched from the first-floor window as the small girl emerged from the shadow of the house, scampering across his lawn to join her friends.

'Do you want the children punished?'

Morton turned to the white-coated figure at his shoulder.

'Of course not!' he snapped. 'They are important to us, Peyne, remember that. As long as our "guests" were not disturbed.'

'They sleep. The medication ensures that.'

'Last night's test was successful?'

'Satisfactory. Do you need help returning to the lower levels?'

'I can manage!'

The figure gave a shrug and turned from the window. 'Then I shall return to my duties.'

Morton watched with distaste as the figure left, the white coat gleaming in the dark of the room. It was like watching a ghost. Dust swirled from the floorboards, leaving footprints clearly visible in a trail to the door. Morton sighed. It had been a long time since anyone had cared about the appearance of the house. Certainly his 'colleagues' had no interest in its upkeep. It was a place in which to work, a place for them to finish what had been started so long ago.

Morton gripped the arms of his ancient wheelchair. A place for them to finish it. And he so desperately wanted it to be finished.

He pushed himself away from the window, wheels squealing on the wooden floor, and moved away from the light and into the gloom of the house.

Rose and the Doctor strode up the hill towards the rectory, the Doctor munching on a slice of toast. He'd already had a gargantuan breakfast and Rose couldn't believe he was still eating.

Her night had been an unsettled one, though the room was comfortable enough. The Hardys were obviously used to making their guests feel at home and Rose had been given a small, cosy attic room, with low beams supporting the ceiling and soft pillows on the bed.

But the night had been full of strange noises: a girl crying in her sleep – Rose had assumed that was Ali – and deeper, more unfamiliar sounds carried on the wind. Creatures stalking the woods and cliff tops. She had lain there, listening to the roars. It was unbelievable really, monsters prowling a seaside town and the locals accepting it as if it was something normal. But then, so much of her life these days was unbelievable.

She had eventually fallen into a troubled sleep in the early hours of the morning, only to be woken what seemed like minutes later by the Doctor hammering energetically on her door and shouting for her to stir her stumps.

Groaning, Rose had dragged herself out of bed and trudged downstairs a little later to find the Doctor in the restaurant. He was tucking into a huge cooked breakfast, bright-eyed and eager, the morning papers spread out on the table in front of him. Rose had slumped down opposite him, pouring herself a huge mug of coffee from the jug on the table.

'You're one of those annoying people who actually like mornings, aren't you?' she said accusingly, helping herself to some toast from the rack.

The Doctor had grinned at her. 'The creatures only seem to turn up after dark, so we need to make the most of the available daylight! Besides, young Ali and her friends were up and out hours ago, and I want to see if we can catch up with them.'

Rose had been surprised. 'They let her go out on her own?'

The Doctor had just shrugged. 'They know the days are safe. They've started to build these creatures into their normal routine. Humans are adaptable like that.'

'Looks like you had a productive night.' Rose nodded at the dismantled phone that was spread out across one of the pub tables.

'Trying to get a fix on that interference. Haven't traced it yet, but give me time.'

The Doctor had continued to eat until Rose was certain that he was going to burst. Then he jumped to his feet, wiped the egg yolk from his plate with another piece of toast and announced that it was time to pay Nathaniel Morton a visit. Beth had told them the best way to get up to the rectory and the two of them had set off in bright morning sunlight.

Daylight made the village look completely different. Shops were open, locals were out in the street buying groceries, boats bobbed in the little harbour. A normal Welsh fishing village.

They made their way up the hill, past the estate they had passed through the previous night. The rectory was just visible now on a jutting strip of headland, bordered by a long, high wall and towering beech trees.

Rose turned and looked back at the view. Out in the bay the lighthouse loomed from its tangle of black rock, seagulls swirling around it. It made her shiver. While daylight made everything else look cheerier, it somehow accentuated the lighthouse's brooding presence.

'Come on! No time for gawping!' said the Doctor indistinctly through a final mouthful of toast.

'I wasn't gawping at the view, I was looking at the lighthouse,' said Rose indignantly. 'I thought you were planning on getting out there.'

'Yes, that's next on the list, but I want to see Mr

Morton first. Got a gut feeling about him.'

Laughter suddenly cut through the morning air and a gang of half a dozen children ranging in age from about ten to about twelve barrelled around the corner, almost cannoning into them.

The children skidded to a halt. At once the laughter stopped and they stared at the Doctor and Rose suspiciously, their faces a mixture of bravado and fear, a look that Rose recognised from all children who have just been caught doing something they shouldn't have.

The Doctor obviously recognised the look too. He stood with his hands thrust deep into the pockets of his coat, staring at them with mock sternness.

'Hello. And where are you lot heading off to in such a hurry?'

One of the older boys, with a tangle of untidy blond hair, looked back at him defiantly. 'None of your business, is it?'

'None at all!' said the Doctor cheerfully. 'I'm just being nosy. Can't help it. See something I don't know about, have to stick my hooter in!'

There was the patter of feet and more high-pitched laughter, and two other figures hared into view. It was Ali with a boy.

'Ah! I might have known,' cried the Doctor. 'Little Ali! It's always the small ones you've got to watch.'

'I'm not small!' Ali frowned.

The boy with her clenched his fists. 'She doesn't like being called small.'

Rose stifled a smile. 'He's keen,' she muttered.

The boy obviously heard her and reddened. 'Do you know him?' he asked.

Ali nodded. 'He's a doctor. He's staying with Mum and Dad. That's Rose.' Ali gave her a shy smile.

The kids suddenly looked worried and the blond boy took a step backwards.

'What've they called a doctor for? We don't need any doctor.'

The Doctor shook his head. 'I'm not *any* doctor, I'm THE Doctor. Completely different. We're off to investigate the rectory. A lady called Bronwyn thinks it might have something to do with the creatures in the woods. What do you think?'

The children shuffled awkwardly again.

'Dunno what you mean.' The blond boy wouldn't meet the Doctor's gaze.

'Really?' The Doctor dropped on to his haunches, bringing him head height with Ali. ''Cause Ali here certainly does, and she's not remotely scared of talking about them.'

'I'm not scared.' The boy was angry again. 'Not scared of the monsters or you or them at the rectory!'

'So you've been there?'

The boy clenched his jaw. 'Maybe.'

'We play dare,' piped up Ali. 'We've all done it now.

Even me. Knocking at the door. Hiding from them.'

'Hiding from who?' asked Rose.

Ali shrugged. 'Dunno who they are. They wear masks. Like in hospital. And white coats. We've seen…'

The boy standing next to her dug her in the ribs with his elbow and she stopped.

'Seen what?' Rose crouched down next to the Doctor. 'What have you seen? You can tell us, honest.'

Ali looked around her friends, then shook her head. 'Nothing.'

'Come on. What are we hanging around here for?' And with that the blond boy set off down the hill at a jog, shouting back over his shoulder, 'He's not a teacher or our parents. We don't have to talk to him.'

The rest of the gang started to run after him, Ali with them. She stopped and looked back at Rose for a moment, then hurried to catch up her friends.

Rose straightened. 'She *so* wants to tell us something.'

'She did tell us something. Figures at the rectory with surgical masks dressed in white lab coats.'

'The people you saw last night, by the sea!'

'Yes.' The Doctor nodded. 'Come on. Let's see if we can play dare too.'

The two of them set off along the narrow lane again. Before long they turned a corner and there were the gates of the rectory, tall and imposing. And unlocked.

They didn't look as though they had been used for years, ivy and brambles twining through the rusted iron bars. Beyond them they could see the house itself at the end of a curving gravel drive.

'Very nice!' The Doctor was impressed. 'Old Nathaniel's definitely a local boy made good, eh?'

Rose grimaced and crunched up the drive after the Doctor. The house was cold and dour-looking, enough to give the kids nightmares with or without monsters. There was a flicker of movement at the edge of her vision and she looked up in time to see heavy curtains on the first floor swing back into place. She hurried over to join the Doctor on the porch.

'Someone knows we're here.'

'Good. Not much point in coming all this way to find no one at home.'

The Doctor grasped the heavy brass knocker and rapped forcefully on the door. From inside Rose could hear the sound of movement, footsteps on a hard floor, and then, with a clatter of keys and bolts, the door swung open.

An imposing thin-faced woman in a pristine white lab coat stood in the doorway, regarding them imperiously.

The Doctor held out a hand, grinning from ear to ear. 'Good morning. I'm Dr… Jones… and this is my PA, Miss… Evans. We have an appointment to see Nathaniel Morton.'

The woman looked at the Doctor's outstretched hand with distaste, making no move to take it. 'An appointment?'

'Well, I say appointment. It's not *exactly* an appointment… it's not like we booked it with his secretary or anything. You're not his secretary, are you?'

The woman glared at him.

'Course you're not. Silly of me. Well, it's a bit more informal than that. Less of an appointment, more of a 'drop by if you're passing' sort of thing. Not that Mr Morton said that as such, it's just we were passing and we thought we'd drop by…' The Doctor tailed off. 'He does actually live here, doesn't he? Mr Morton?'

'I'll deal with this, thank you, Miss Peyne.'

With a squeak of tyres, an ancient wheelchair rolled from the shadows. The man sitting in it was pale and gaunt, with wisps of grey hair lying untidily over his head. The wheelchair slid to a halt and the man looked up at the Doctor quizzically.

'I'm Nathaniel Morton. You have business with me?'

His voice was weak and wavering but his eyes blazed with a fierce intelligence and Rose got the impression of someone very dangerous trapped within that frail body.

The Doctor pulled the wallet holding his psychic paper from his pocket and handed it to Morton. 'Dr Jones. From Cardiff. Conducting a survey of medical facilities in the area. Surprise inspection. Hope you don't mind.'

Morton took the wallet and studied the paper. There was a long awkward pause and Rose held her breath. Then Morton abruptly snapped the wallet closed and handed it back to the Doctor.

'You'd better come into my office.'

Gripping the wheels of the wheelchair, Morton spun it on the spot and rolled back into the gloom of the house. The Doctor and Rose followed. There was a loud bang as the door slammed behind them and the clatter of keys in the lock as Miss Peyne locked the door.

Rose tugged at the Doctor's sleeve. 'Didn't think it was going to work that time!' she whispered.

'Yes, wasn't sure myself for a moment. And I don't think Miss Peyne was too keen about letting us in.'

'God, she couldn't have a better name! How scary was she!'

'I know!'

They followed Morton down the dark hallway, their footsteps echoing off the high ceilings. At the end of the passage was a wide staircase, with weak light filtering through a tall window on the landing. Rose jumped as two pale figures padded down the stairs, their faces hidden by surgical masks, long lab coats flapping behind them. There was an unpleasant smell of disinfectant as the figures hurried past them, vanishing down another corridor. Rose shivered. She didn't like places like this. It reminded her of the old people's home her gran had had to go in for a little while before she died: a stale, soulless place full of people with dead eyes and no hope. Her mum had made her promise that she'd never put her in a place like that.

Morton rolled to a halt in front of a heavy oak door and pushed it open, gesturing for the Doctor and Rose to enter. They stepped through into a large, gloomy office. The walls were mostly lined with bookcases that groaned under the weight of heavy tomes and dust motes glinted in the shafts of weak sunlight that cut across the room.

Wheeling himself across to a large wooden desk, Morton shuffled papers to one side. Rose glanced around the room nervously. The walls that were free of books were hung with huge, ugly paintings. Jars with strange twisted forms stood on glass-fronted cabinets and trays of surgical instruments gleamed on tables.

'Sit down please, Dr… Jones, Miss Evans, and tell me what I can do for you.' Morton regarded them balefully.

The Doctor slid into one of the old leather chairs, seemingly quite at home.

'We're interested in the work you're doing here, Mr Morton. And the effect it might be having on the local community.'

'This is a rest home for the elderly, Doctor, nothing more.'

'An unusual place for a retirement home, surely? A bit out of the way?'

'The clients in my care are wealthy. They have a desire for solitude, somewhere they can spend the twilight years of their life without prying eyes and unwelcome questions.' The threat in his voice was obvious. 'As for any effect on the community, I'm sure I don't know what you mean.'

'One of the locals seems to think that whatever you're doing here is affecting the well-being of their children. You don't exactly seem to have gone out of your way to fit in. I can't really see you and Miss Peyne joining in the local darts night down at the Red Lion.'

'This community is averse to change, Doctor, to anything new. And forgive me, but if I wish to keep myself to myself that is hardly any concern of yours.'

'And the noise of ravenous creatures roaming the hills doesn't disturb the rest of your *clients* at all?' Rose chipped in.

Morton gave a blustering laugh. 'Creatures? Really, young lady…'

'And the death of a young man on the shore, that's no worry to you either?' The Doctor's voice was harsh now.

Morton's smile faded.

'If there had been such a death, then it would be a matter for the police and not for a doctor.'

The two men glared at each other across the desk for a moment, then the Doctor broke into a broad smile.

'Quite right!' He rose from his seat. 'Well, thank you for your time, Mr Morton. Most helpful. I hope that we haven't disturbed you too much with our unwelcome questions. Miss Evans…'

The Doctor hauled Rose from her seat and thrust her towards the door. Morton struggled to extricate his wheelchair from behind the desk. The Doctor waved a hand at him.

'Please don't bother showing us out. I'm sure we can find our own way.' He bundled Rose out of the door into the hallway. 'This is right, isn't it?' he called back over his shoulder.

They hurried along the dark passage, heading past the staircase and down another corridor. In the distance they could hear the ringing of a bell – a relic of the time when the house was full of servants, no doubt – and Morton's voice calling for Miss Peyne.

'Did you see which door those two in the masks went into?' asked the Doctor.

'This one, I think.' Rose pointed at an ornate oak door.

'That's what I thought too.'

There was a flare of blue light and a high-pitched whine as the Doctor pressed his sonic screwdriver to the lock. The door swung open and they slipped through into the room beyond.

Rose stared in horror at the room before her. It was long and high-ceilinged. Tall windows lined one wall and an elaborate chandelier hung from an elegant ceiling rose. It had obviously been a dining room of some kind for the rectory's previous owners, but Nathaniel Morton had found another use for it.

The tall windows were shuttered and dark, the chandelier disused and covered in cobwebs. Beds lined the walls, bathed in pools of soft light from concealed sources. Stacks of gleaming medical machinery hummed and bleeped quietly, while transparent tubes and arm-thick cables snaked their way across the scuffed and faded parquet floor and along the peeling skirting.

But it was the figures in the beds that made Rose stop and stare.

Six of them, silent and motionless, faces pale even against the white of the sheets and pillows, their breathing shallow and faint. Four men, two women: old, no, *ancient*, their skin almost transparent, their hair wispy and silver. Thin, positively skeletal hands rested on the blankets covering them, while needles protruded obscenely from their veins. The entire room smelt antiseptic, clinical.

White-coated figures padded softly from bed to bed,

adjusting tubes, peering at machines, their faces masked and anonymous. The Doctor and Rose walked between the beds, watching as one of the nurses – if that's what they were – jotted down a set of readings from one of the machines.

'What are they doing to them?' Rose whispered.

The Doctor shook his head. 'I'm not sure.'

When he moved as if to examine a sleeping figure, the white-coated attendants immediately turned as one, pushing him backwards.

The Doctor held his hands up. 'All right, all right, I was only looking. I wasn't going to touch.'

The door behind them swung open again and Rose turned to see Miss Peyne pushing Morton down the length of the room. The old man had a face like thunder.

'What are you doing in here?' he hissed.

The Doctor tried his best to look apologetic. 'Took a wrong turn. Sorry about that. Thought we were heading for the front door and ended up here.'

'You have no right to be in here. No right at all!' Morton was almost shaking with fury. 'You could have caused incalculable damage.'

Rose suddenly felt guilty. Perhaps this *was* just a nursing home after all.

'Look, we didn't touch anything. But what's going on here? Who are these people?'

'No business of yours!' snapped Morton. 'As I told

you, we came here for seclusion and that is what we want. Seclusion. Now, get out! Both of you!'

The Doctor shot a quick glance at Rose, then nodded. 'Of course. Sorry for the intrusion.'

Morton just glowered at him.

The Doctor shrugged and, with a final glance round the room, ushered Rose back out into the hallway.

Miss Peyne followed, closing the door behind them. She gestured to her left and when she spoke, her voice was like ice. 'The front door is this way, Doctor. Miss Evans.'

The Doctor smiled at her. 'So easy to get lost in these big houses, isn't it?'

'Yes, indeed. They can be dangerous places if you're not careful.'

They walked in silence to the front door. When they got there, Miss Peyne pulled a heavy key from a chain around her neck, unlocked the door and slid back the bolts.

'I trust you'll be able to find your way to the end of the drive without any further assistance.'

The Doctor and Rose stepped back out into the morning light, blinking after the gloom of the rectory. The door slammed with a loud thump and they could hear the bolts being slid back into place.

The Doctor looked at Rose with indignation. 'Was that a threat? It sounded like a threat. I'm not sure we deserved to be threatened, are you?'

'Oh no, not at all.' Rose rolled her eyes. 'We did a runner from his office, unlocked his secret hospital ward and had a nose about without his permission. Don't see what he was getting all worked up about.'

'Exactly! And you know another thing? I've got no idea what he saw in the psychic paper. Not a clue. Normally I get some kind of after-image, but this time, not a sausage. Odd. Definitely odd.'

'So, d'you think it's got something to do with the creatures?'

'Do I think?' The Doctor turned and looked back at the rectory. 'Oh, I'm certain of it.'

Nathaniel Morton watched from his office window as the Doctor and his companion turned away from the house and trudged down the drive and out of sight. He heard the door open behind him and Miss Peyne joined him at the window.

'You were foolish, Morton, letting him get into the ward like that.'

'You think I had a choice?' Morton snapped. 'You think I could have done anything more to stop him?'

'Who was he?'

'He claimed to be a government inspector, but…'

'But what?'

'The credentials he showed me. The paper. It was a mind trick of some kind.'

'You think he's on to us?' Peyne's voice was anxious.

'If he was, he'd never have been so direct. No, this one is something different.'

'We should dispose of him.'

'We can't risk it! Another death so soon after the last one will attract attention. And this one would be missed. No, we'll bide our time with the mysterious Dr Jones. By the time he does figure out what's going on it will be too late, and if he does return to the house, well, next time we won't be so accommodating.'

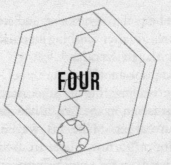

FOUR

The Doctor sat on the harbour wall, eating an ice-cream cone and staring out at the lighthouse. The brief glimpse he'd got of the equipment at the rectory had convinced him that there was far more going on in that ward than just caring for six elderly people, but he needed more time to study it and there was no way that Morton was going to let them in again in a hurry. Hopefully Rose would help in that regard.

The two of them had headed back to the pub for lunch, working out their best plan of attack. The Doctor had been determined to get a fix on whatever was jamming the phone lines. The signal was complex and it had taken him some time to pin down its source.

Perhaps unsurprisingly, it seemed to be coming from the lighthouse, but it was a waste of their resources for them both to go out there. Instead, Rose could do a bit of snooping at the rectory while he concentrated on the lighthouse and its mysterious transmissions. So, after finishing lunch, she had set off in search of Ali and the other kids.

The Doctor took another mouthful of his ice cream, checked the readings on his sonic screwdriver and regarded the island in the bay. It had seemed such a simple plan earlier. Make his way down to the harbour, hire or borrow a boat from some friendly fisherman, head out for a quick shufty, sorted.

Unfortunately, there were no boats out in the harbour. The fishing boats were all out catching fish and late September wasn't exactly tourist season, so all the boats that offered trips round the bay and visits to Black Island were beached for the winter.

Bob Perry, the harbour master, had a little motorboat – the Doctor could see it tied up at the end of the jetty – but Bob had made it perfectly plain that the boat was for 'official business only' and he wasn't in the mood to discuss the matter further. In the end, the Doctor had just bought a postcard and an ice cream off him instead, the harbour master's office seemingly doubling as a gift shop.

Wandering back along the harbour wall, the Doctor had toyed with the idea of unchaining one of the little pleasure boats from the prom and trying to launch it himself, but the chances of getting it unlocked and into the water without being challenged by someone were remote. He had even thought about taking one of the swan-shaped pedal boats from the duck pond in the local park, but upon reflection they had looked less than seaworthy.

He gave a deep sigh and scanned the horizon, looking for further options. A glint of colour on the far side of the harbour caught his eye. He stuffed the remnants of his ice-cream cone into his mouth and pulled out his opera glasses, adjusting the fingertip controls on either side and bringing the little LCD screens into sharp focus.

On a short stretch of shingle beach the prow of a small fishing boat protruded from beneath a faded tarpaulin, the name *Jimmy* picked out in red paint.

'Gotcha.'

Popping the glasses back into his pocket, the Doctor hopped down off the wall and headed back to the harbour master's office.

Bob Perry looked up from his paper suspiciously as the Doctor rapped cheerfully on his door.

'Oh, it's you again. Wanting another ice cream, are you? Still not cold enough?'

He reached for a large chest freezer under the counter, the signs for ice creams and ice lollies and the racks of picture postcards incongruous among the port authority notices and life-saving equipment.

'No, no, no. No more for me. I'll spoil my dinner. I was wondering if you knew who the boat on the beach just over there belongs to.' The Doctor pointed at the little shingle beach. 'Boat called *Jimmy*.'

Bob settled back down into his chair. 'That'll be Bronwyn Ceredig's boat.'

'Is it for hire?'

'Still trying to get out to Black Island, are you? Well, you can ask, but I can't promise you'll get a sensible answer from her.'

'She didn't seem the most popular lady last night in the pub.'

'Popular?' Bob gave a contemptuous laugh. 'She's mad as a box of frogs, that one. Lives in a right mess of a house on the west beach. Local council's been trying to move her on for years. Bad for the tourist business, see? So she's about as popular as a fart in a spacesuit.'

'Yeah, that is unpleasant.' The Doctor nodded thoughtfully. 'Think there's any chance she'd hire the boat to me?'

'For a price, maybe, if she likes your face. But whatever happens, don't let her offer to take you out there herself. I've had enough trouble with her and that boat over the last year, and I really don't want to have to leave my nice cosy office to tow her back to shore again because she's put herbal shampoo instead of engine oil in her outboard motor again.'

'Shampoo?' The Doctor's hearts began to sink.

'Herbal shampoo. Lavender and tea tree oil, I think it was. Thought it would be better for the environment. She's very concerned about the seals.'

'The seals…'

'Colony of them out on the island. You might see them if you're lucky. Have a nice trip.'

Bob raised his paper again, settling back into his chair, smirking.

The Doctor gave a deep sigh. The day was getting on and he had to make his way out to the lighthouse and back before darkness fell. He was running out of options.

'Bronwyn it is, then. Let's just hope she's out of shampoo.'

Rose was starting to get frustrated. The visit to the rectory had piqued the Doctor's curiosity and he wanted to know more about both the ward and the mysterious masked figures that operated it. He had asked Rose to find the gang of kids they had met earlier. They had obviously seen more goings-on at the rectory than they cared to talk about, but it was becoming clear that Ali wanted to tell them something and the Doctor was certain that if she was going to talk to anyone, then it was going to be Rose.

It had suited Rose fine. She liked it when the Doctor relied on her. Besides, how tricky could it be? Finding half a dozen bored kids in a place as small as Ynys Du? No problem.

The trouble was they were nowhere to be seen. Rose was baffled. When she was that age, she and her friends had hung about the shops, or the cinema, or that scrap of waste ground round the back of the estate that someone had tried to turn into a kid's playground. Ynys Du was a very different place from the Powell Estate, though. The only shops to speak of sold groceries or catered for the tourist trade. There was no cinema and the playground was desolate, windswept and locked. She had been wandering around the village for nearly an hour now. What the hell did kids do in a place like this when there was no school?

Having exhausted all the possibilities in the village, Rose started to think about where else they might have gone. Her mind drifted back to the modern estate that she and the Doctor had come through when they first arrived. Perhaps some of the kids lived up there and they were playing football in one of the gardens. None of the little terraced houses in the village had gardens, so it was a possibility.

Pleased with her logic, Rose set off at a brisk pace, trying to get some warmth back into her bones. It wasn't raining but the air was damp and the wind off the sea was threatening to bring more bad weather as the day went on. The sooner she found those kids and got back to the warmth of the pub the better.

The road winding up from the village was steeper than she remembered and soon she had to unzip her heavy parka despite the chill air. She crested the hill panting. God, you'd have thought with all the corridors she'd had to run down over the last few months she'd be fitter than this!

Catching her breath, she wandered towards the cul-de-sac where the Doctor had frightened off the monsters the previous night. It all looked so different in daylight. A normal, boring housing estate, the same as thousands of others across the country; well kept, quiet and disappointingly free of the sound of children playing.

Rose cursed under her breath. A man out in his driveway, cleaning his car, was watching her suspiciously. She smiled at him in what she hoped was a disarming and friendly way and kept walking. She'd do a quick circuit of the area, just in case.

A gust of wind sent a ripple through the trees at the edge of the estate, dead leaves swirling across the road. Rose struggled with the zip of her parka again. Daylight had had no friendly, softening effect on the wood, which still clung to the hillside, dark and ominous. Rose peered into the darkness. Surely the kids weren't stupid enough to be playing in there?

She turned away, intending to head back down to the village, when she caught the sound of laughter through the trees. The kids *were* playing in the woods!

Suddenly the prospect of exploring the lighthouse with the Doctor seemed the better option to Rose. Wishing that she had a couple of his everlasting matches with her, Rose stepped into the wood, straining to hear where the laughter was coming from. She crept forward, wincing at each rustle of leaves or crack of dead branches. The laughter had been replaced by whispered conversation and loud ssshhs now, and Rose could smell wood smoke.

A loud crack made her jump and, in an explosion of wet leaves and thrashing undergrowth, a figure in baggy jeans and a sweatshirt burst from the trees in front of her, tearing through the wood and vanishing into the safety of the estate. From where the figure had emerged, Rose could see a jumble of corrugated-iron sheets, badly camouflaged with dead branches. A wisp of smoke curled into the air from behind it before being whipped away by the wind.

Rose peered over the corrugated iron and five frightened faces looked up at her. She gave a deep sigh of relief.

'I told you it wasn't a monster!' One of the girls punched a boy on the shoulder, the boy Rose had seen Ali with earlier. 'I told you! They only come out at night, don't they?'

The boy glowered at Rose before saying, 'Nearly gave us a heart attack.'

Rose laughed nervously. 'You and me both! Who was doing the world speed record?'

'That was Dai Barraclough.' Ali was smiling. 'I think he wet himself.'

The kids dissolved into giggles. Rose slipped round the corrugated-iron sheeting and crouched down next to Ali. The kids had made a crude shelter in the lea of a tall oak tree. A small pile of wet twigs smoked fitfully and the floor was strewn with sweet wrappers and drinks cans.

'This is where you all hang out?' asked Rose.

Ali nodded. 'It's our hideout. We're a gang. You've got to do the dare to join.'

'Well, it looks like I'm a member, then.'

Ali's eyes widened. 'You went into the house?'

Rose nodded. 'Uh-huh. Saw Mr Morton and his creepy nurses.'

'Really?' Ali was obviously impressed.

'Yeah, really. And if I'm a member of your gang, then I hope you don't need to keep secrets from me.'

Ali regarded her for a moment, then stood up. 'We'll need to take a vote.'

She motioned to her friends to follow her and the five children went into a huddle on the other side of the clearing. There was a lot of loud whispering, then Ali turned and came back to where Rose was sitting.

'We've decided you can join. I told them that you're OK, that we can trust you.'

'Thank you.' Rose smiled.

'But not your friend. He's too old.'

Rose giggled. 'You're more right than you know!'

The other children joined them.

Ali pointed at each in turn. 'That's Baz Morgan. He lives in one of the new houses. We play football at his house sometimes. The girls are Sian and Jane Evans. Their mum runs the baker's. Dai is the boy who ran off. You talked to him this morning.'

Rose nodded. The blond kid with the attitude. She wasn't sad to see the back of him.

'Yeah, didn't think he liked me.'

'And this is Billy Palmer.' Ali pushed her friend forward. 'He saw stuff at the rectory.'

Rose held out her hand. 'Hello.'

Billy shook it solemnly. 'Hi.'

'What sort of stuff did you see?'

Billy shrugged. 'Just vans at first, delivering stuff. Equipment. Computers and things. Then the people in the masks appeared. Didn't see them arrive... They were just there one morning. Me and Dai had snuck into the courtyard at the back, were trying to see through the window into the cellar. They nearly saw me. Had to hide behind the bins. That's when I saw the bad stuff.'

'Bad stuff?' Rose felt the hairs on her neck stand up. 'What sort of bad stuff?'

Billy looked nervously round at his friends. 'Bags. Black bin bags. But there was a smell and... red stuff. One of the bags was leaking and I saw red stuff come out.'

'Blood?' Rose thought back to the pools of blood on

the shore, the Doctor's suspicion that someone was 'cleaning up after their pet'.

'I think so. We didn't hang around to find out. We legged it for the tunnel.'

'Tunnel?'

'We found it,' announced Ali proudly. 'None of the grown-ups know it's there. Going down the tunnel's another dare.' Her face fell. 'Only Billy and Dai have been brave enough to go down it so far.'

Rose's mind was racing. She wasn't certain that Ali was right about them being the only ones who knew about the mysterious tunnel. Parents did tend to know more about what their children got up to than they let on. But whether Morton knew about the tunnel was another matter. He certainly had no interest in the upkeep of the house and the fact that the kids were able to get into the grounds via some secret entrance probably meant that he had even less of an interest in the history of the property.

It seemed the perfect way to get a closer look at the house without Morton knowing.

'Can you tell me where this tunnel is?'

'Sure.' Ali caught hold of her hand. 'It's this way. Come on. I'll show you.'

The Doctor trudged down the shingle towards an extraordinary tangle of rubbish piled up on the beach. From a distance it looked like a heap of flotsam deposited by a particularly high tide, but as he drew closer he could see that there was some kind of method to the madness, glimpses of what must once have been some sort of large beach house or holiday home protruding through the debris.

Tarpaulins stretched out over the roof were held in place with clumsy clusters of knotted rope, walls were patched with pieces of driftwood and the sides of packing crates, window frames were splintered and rotten, and from a tall metal pipe towering over the structure a thin trail of smoke emerged, whipped inland by the offshore breeze.

Behind the house what had once been a sizeable fenced garden was now a jumble of salvage from the sea. Oil drums, plastic buoys, fishing nets and lobster pots lay among huge piles of driftwood, with brambles snaking through them. A wreath of lifebelts hung on the twisted remnants of a children's swing, and underneath everything the Doctor could just make out the shape of what looked like an old Triumph Herald, its bodywork rusted and corroded after years in the sea air.

From inside came the sound of singing and the smell of cooking. The Doctor stepped up to the shabby front door, straightened his coat and knocked firmly. There was a muffled curse from inside, followed by the sound of movement. A few moments later the patched and battered door swung open and Bronwyn Ceredig peered out at him suspiciously with those brilliant grey eyes of hers. She was wearing a long floral dress, with a striped apron tied around her waist. Her long grey hair was pulled back in an untidy bun and little half-moon spectacles perched precariously on the tip of her nose.

'Yes?'

The Doctor smiled his broadest smile.

'Good afternoon! Bronwyn, isn't it? I'm the Doctor. We met at the pub last night. Bob over at the harbour said that you might be the best person to talk to about hiring a boat!'

She gave a disdainful sniff, threw the door open and vanished back into the house. 'You'd better come in. I'm just making some Welsh cakes.'

The Doctor followed her, closing the door behind him.

The inside of the house was, if anything, more of a mess than the outside. Books, ornaments and photographs covered every surface, while the floor was piled high with newspapers and magazines, and pictures hung on every wall. Among the chaos protruded furniture, the covers faded and torn. The pleasant smell of cooking filled the air from a small kitchenette.

Bronwyn waved at him from in front of the stove. 'Clear yourself a space and sit down. Watch out for the duck.'

The Doctor stepped warily into the room. A large mallard eyed him from its position on the couch. Moving a box of shoes, the Doctor sat down carefully next to it.

Bronwyn bustled out of the kitchenette, a plate of Welsh cakes in her hand. She thrust the plate at the Doctor, taking one herself.

'I remember you now. Said that you were here to help.'

'That's right.'

She glowered at him. 'How?'

'Well, for starters I wanted to ask you about Nathaniel Morton. You don't seem to have much time for him.'

'He's messing with things best left alone.'

'You mean the creatures?'

'I know what I mean.' She took another mouthful of cake. 'You said Bob sent you over? So you'll be wanting to hire the boat?'

'That's right. Want to get out to the island.'

'Why do you want to head out there?'

'Erm… To see the seals?' The Doctor took a bite of his Welsh cake, ignoring the greedy eye of the duck.

Bronwyn nodded, as if that explained everything.

The Doctor went on, 'I gather that the island is the best place to see them.'

'That's true. And you're in luck. I was planning on heading out there myself.'

She undid her apron and threw it into the corner, then fed the remains of her Welsh cake to the duck, which swallowed them greedily.

'You wait there, Dr whoever-you-are. I won't be a minute.'

She pushed her way through the tangle of boxes to another door on the far side of the room. Hoping that she wasn't collecting any shampoo, the Doctor picked up a stack of photos from the table alongside him and started flicking idly through them.

Almost all of them were in black and white, showing the village as it had been. From the look of things, not that much had changed over the last fifty years or so. The harbour was just the same, the seafront dominated by the imposing Victorian façade of the pub, the street leading up the hill still lined with the same cluster of small shop fronts, only the signage in the windows and the price tags visible on stalls giving the age of the photographs away. There were shots of the lighthouse in the bay, the paintwork clean and fresh, the lighthouse keepers posing proudly on the rocks at its base. There was even a photo of the rectory, its gardens neatly kept and the shrubbery that now grew wild trimmed and orderly.

As the Doctor looked through the photographs he realised that a lot of them featured Bronwyn as a young woman. She had been attractive in her youth, with long auburn hair cascading over her shoulders and a smile on her face in every picture.

One photograph showed her standing outside the beach house, a young man at her shoulder, a baby in her arms. The house was tidy and whitewashed, a line full of clean clothes hanging alongside it. Another showed the three of them on the beach, only this time the baby had grown into a small boy in shorts, his knees covered in sand, a bucket and spade being waved enthusiastically at the photographer.

The Doctor put the photographs down and stared around the room. Nearly all of the photos on the walls or in frames on the top of cupboards featured the boy. He must have been five or six years old at a guess.

Hauling himself out of the sagging sofa, the Doctor slipped on his glasses. A jumble of photographs of the boy in a smart school uniform sat propped up against a vase on one of the groaning shelves. He picked them up, peering at them one by one. The boy had the same bright eyes and slightly crooked smile as his mother.

'Where are you now, I wonder?' he murmured.

Plucking one of them from the pile, the Doctor slipped it into his jacket pocket.

At that moment Bronwyn bustled back into the room. She was now wearing a huge battered oilskin and had a canvas bag slung over her shoulder. The Doctor hurriedly tried to put the rest of the photographs back in their place, fumbling and dropping several on to the floor. Flashing her a guilty grin, he gathered them up.

'Sorry. Butterfingers.'

Bronwyn snatched the photographs from him, putting them back in their place. The Doctor watched as her fingers ran gently over the pictures.

'Good-looking boy.'

A flicker of a smile started to cross her face, taking years off her. 'Yes…'

The smile vanished as suddenly as it had arrived and she shot the Doctor a suspicious glance.

'We'd better get a move on if we're going to catch the tide,' she said.

'Absolutely. Don't want to keep those seals waiting.'

Bronwyn bustled out of the room, muttering to herself. The Doctor took off his spectacles and fingered the photograph in his pocket. Something dark had happened in Bronwyn's past, of that he had no doubt. Something to do with her son. It could not have been a coincidence that Rose had seen a child in her dream. It could also not have been a coincidence that there was history between Bronwyn and Nathaniel Morton. The problem was that he was still no closer to finding out what.

He tapped his teeth thoughtfully with the arm of his glasses.

'Jimmy,' he murmured.

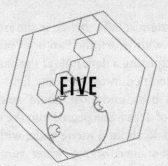

FIVE

'There you are!' Ali pointed proudly at a low pile of ruined brickwork that emerged from under a sprawling holly bush.

She and the others had led Rose through the wood until they came to the high, imposing wall that bordered the back of the rectory grounds. Then they had followed the wall until they reached what had once been outbuildings serving the main house. Here the kids had scrambled enthusiastically underneath the foliage.

Rose pushed her way forward through the tangle of branches to where Billy Palmer and Baz Morgan were clearing leaves from a sheet of rotten plywood. The ruined building had obviously been a coal house or storeroom of some kind. The remains of bunkers could be seen among the vegetation and ancient rusted rail tracks snaked off through the wood, vanishing in the undergrowth, evidence of the industry that must have thrived in the area in the past.

Grunting with effort, the two boys pulled back the plywood, exposing a dark hole at the base of the wall. Woodlice scuttled away from the light as the board was pulled back and Rose could smell the damp muskiness of decay. She peered into the tunnel. It was made of brick, about a metre wide, with a stream of murky, rust-stained orange water running down a drain in its centre.

Ali hunkered down next to her and peered into the tunnel, wrinkling her nose.

'It smells a bit, but it's quite safe.'

'Yeah! Like you'd know,' snorted Billy. 'You've not been down there.'

'But you have?' Rose looked at him.

Billy nodded. 'Like I said, it goes under the wall, comes up at the back of the house, in a kind of courtyard next to the cellars.'

'How long is it?'

Billy shrugged. 'Dunno. Not far.' He paused. 'Do you want me to show you?'

Rose smiled at the nervousness in the boy's voice. He obviously didn't want to go down the tunnel again, but equally he didn't want to lose face with his friends. She shook her head.

'Nah. It's OK.'

'I'll go with you!' piped up Ali.

'No! I want you to stay here. All of you.' She looked

around the little group. 'I need you to make sure no one comes in behind me. And if I don't come back out in about half an hour, go and find the Doctor back at the pub. All right?'

The kids nodded, relieved that Rose hadn't asked them to go with her.

Ali pouted and crossed her arms. 'It's not fair!'

Rose looked at her sternly. 'I mean it, Ali. I need you to keep an eye on things at this end.' She squeezed her arm. 'I'll be ten minutes, OK?'

Ali nodded.

With more bravado than she felt, Rose gave the watching children a reassuring smile, took a deep breath and ducked into the tunnel. There was a moment of panic when she realised that she wouldn't be able to stand up straight, but the floor was so slippery with moss and slime that that wouldn't have been a good idea anyway. Instead she pressed her hands against the roof and walls to keep her balance and started to edge her way forward.

The tunnel was dark and with every step she took away from the entrance the blackness deepened. She strained to make out any shapes in the gloom ahead of her, but there was nothing. She glanced back over her shoulder. Five faces framed the tunnel entrance, watching her progress. Determined not to let them or the Doctor down, Rose headed deeper into the darkness.

* * *

The Doctor stood on the shore of Black Island, hands thrust deep into his coat pockets, staring up in admiration at the lighthouse that loomed over him.

The journey out had been decidedly choppy, as Bronwyn's little motorboat was tossed about like a leaf on the wild sea. It had taken them quite a while to get prepared for the trip. The outboard motor had been in a terrible state and the Doctor had had to practically strip it down and rebuild it before it would start. At least that had impressed Bronwyn, who promised to give him a tin of Welsh cakes to take away with him, and possibly some bara brith too.

They had hauled the boat's trailer across the shingle, finally manoeuvring it to a small concrete ramp at the water's edge. Bronwyn was considerably stronger than she looked, and soon the little boat was bobbing in the surf.

Unperturbed by the icy water, Bronwyn had slipped off her shoes, hitched up her skirt and clambered aboard the boat with apparent ease. The Doctor had been less successful and his trousers were soaked to the knees.

By the time they were under way the day was getting on and the wind had picked up considerably. The waves battered the little boat hard as it cleared the shelter of the harbour. Despite Bob Perry's concerns, Bronwyn had proved herself to be a fairly experienced sailor and soon the boat was chugging determinedly towards the island.

The canvas bag had proved to be full of nothing more than provisions for the local wildlife and Bronwyn hurled handfuls of stale bread into the wind for the seagulls. Before long a huge white cloud of them was shadowing the boat, swooping down each time Bronwyn delved into the bag.

As they approached the island itself, landing had seemed an impossible task to the Doctor. The black rocks were viciously jagged and the waves pounded against them, sending great flumes of spray into the air. Bronwyn was obviously a regular visitor, though, and had steered skilfully round to a long shelf of rock that deflected the bulk of the waves. She had kept the boat hovering just off shore until a lull came in the swell, then gunned the motor and sent them speeding between the rocks to a small sheltered cove.

She was down on the rocks now, tossing fish to where half a dozen seals bobbed in the water. The Doctor had left her to it and headed for the base of the lighthouse.

Wind swept his hair back as he stared up at the tower. It was impressive: tall and tapered, made up of dozens of steel sections held together with hundreds of huge rusted bolts. Paint flaked untidily from the sides and high overhead a rusted walkway circled the lamp room like a collar.

Most of the glass in the lamp room had long since gone and the top now resembled a huge birdcage, an image that was reinforced thanks to the evidence left by hundreds of seabirds that streaked its sides.

What intrigued the Doctor was that it was so obviously unused, with no sign whatever of anyone having been in it for years. The door at the base was bolted and padlocked, and years of corrosion had practically rusted it shut.

'So why was there a glow from the lamp room last night?' he muttered.

Bronwyn wandered over to his side, wiping her hands on her oilskin. 'Thought you were interested in the seals, not the lighthouse.' Her tone was accusing.

'Oh, I am, I am. Seals. Love 'em. Some of my best friends are seals. Great at parties. But I'm also intrigued by this. Isn't it beautiful?'

Bronwyn looked up at the tower and sniffed dismissively. 'S'pose so. In a way.'

'When was it abandoned?'

'Back in the 1970s. Elwyn Merritt was the last keeper. Got themselves a lightship out on the sandbanks now. Shut this one down, didn't they? Always the way. Things change. People move on.'

'And some come back, don't they? Some like Nathaniel Morton.'

Bronwyn said nothing, but the Doctor could see her jaw clench.

'Something happened between you and Morton, didn't it?' The Doctor kept his voice low and gentle. 'Something a long time ago, when you were young. He went away, but you stayed.'

'Shouldn't have come back.' There was anger in Bronwyn's voice. Anger and fear. 'Told him not to come back!'

'Why?' The Doctor was urgent now. 'What happened?'

Bronwyn's anger erupted at the Doctor. 'What's it to you? What good is it going to do to dig up the past again? Best left buried! It's best left buried, all of it! They can't bring him back.' Tears blurred her eyes, then the anger faded for a moment and she wiped her eyes with her sleeve. 'They can't bring him back.'

Sniffing, she turned and hurried away from the Doctor. He called after her but the wind whipped the words away. He rubbed at his chin. He wasn't going to get anything else from Bronwyn at the moment, but everything here was connected somehow. He just had to find the common link.

He did a slow circuit of the lighthouse, looking for anything unusual, but he saw nothing. To the casual observer, it was nothing more sinister than an abandoned lighthouse on a deserted island.

He pulled his sonic screwdriver from his pocket, determined to solve the issue of the glow in the lamp room if nothing else, when Bronwyn suddenly scrambled back into view, pointing down towards the shore.

She struggled to the Doctor's side, breathless and frightened.

He caught her arm, steadying her. 'What is it? What have you found?'

'Down there. In Pillbox Hole.'

'Pillbox Hole?'

'A cave. By the shore. It wasn't there before. Been here hundreds of times, I have.'

'Show me!'

He caught hold of the old lady's hand and the two of them made their way carefully over the wet rocks. They reached the top of a narrow set of crude steps that had been hacked out and Bronwyn pointed down to a narrow crevice at the bottom.

'In there.'

'OK. Wait here a moment.'

The Doctor released her hand and scampered down the stairs. At the shoreline they flattened out, leading through a sea-worn gash in the side of the island. He slipped through the gap carefully, emerging on to a narrow ledge in the side of a tall cave where the wind and waves echoed mournfully, eerily.

The Doctor stared into the cave and grinned. 'Hah! I knew it!'

Floating in the black water in front of him, rising and falling with the swell, was a spacecraft.

* * *

Rose had crept through the tunnel for what seemed like an age and was on the verge of giving up and heading back to Ali and her friends when she felt cold air across her face.

She could still see nothing – the light from the entrance had long since gone as the tunnel had curved slightly and Rose had edged her way forward by feel alone. But now the breeze told her that she was nearly through.

She gave a sigh of relief and tried to rub the crick out of her neck. Being unable to stand was starting to get painful and she wished she could be Ali's height – for the next few minutes at least.

She was about to continue when a noise from behind made her freeze. She held her breath, concentrating on listening, trying to convince herself that it was just her imagination.

The noise came again. A soft scraping on the brickwork. There was something in the tunnel with her! Rose strained to see through the oppressive blackness, suddenly aware of what a stupid idea it had been to head into the tunnel without any form of light.

She could hear something approaching from behind. And there! Lights flickering. Green and red and blue lights, dancing across the wet brick. Rose pressed herself against the wall, aware of how pointless it was.

'Rose?'

Ali's voice was thunderously loud in the confined space. Rose nearly screamed.

'Rose, is that you?'

Ali emerged from the shadows, a tiny torch in her hand. The LEDs in its tip were cycling through the primary colours.

'Ali, you're gonna be the death of me!' Rose could hear the cracks in her voice. 'You've just taken years off my life! What are you doing in here?'

'Sian remembered she had a torch on a keyring. It was free with a magazine.' She held it out to Rose. 'I thought it might help.'

Rose hugged her. 'Thank you. But you shouldn't have come down here. It could be dangerous.'

'None of the others would do it,' Ali said, extricating herself from Rose's grip. She looked embarrassed.

Rose took the little torch from her. The LEDs were bright enough to see the way ahead. She couldn't send Ali back without it and she'd certainly make better time in the remainder of the tunnel with it.

She caught the girl by the hand. 'OK, you can come with me. But you've gotta promise me that you'll do exactly as I tell you, right?'

Ali nodded.

Torch held out in front of them, the two girls headed forward.

The Doctor hopped from rock to rock, dancing out of

the way of waves, examining the spacecraft. It was small and cigar-shaped, about twelve metres long, with ugly, powerful-looking engines hanging from fins at the rear. The surface was a dull silver-grey, etched with alien hieroglyphics. There were no windows visible, but thick black cables arced from underneath the ship and wound their way up the cave walls, vanishing through neat holes in the rock.

He scrambled up on to a large boulder and peered at them. 'No prizes for guessing where they go!'

'Doctor?'

Bronwyn poked her head tentatively into the cave.

'Bronwyn! Lovely! Come and look at what you've found. Smashing little interstellar hopper. Dual plasma-injection engines, toughened duralinium hull with built-in force-shield deflectors, go-faster paint job and probably a CD changer in the boot!'

Bronwyn shuffled forward nervously. 'Are there… are there any…'

'Occupants? Nah! Not round here, at any rate.'

He jumped down from his perch to her side. 'I think that *they* think they've parked somewhere safe. See that?' He pointed at a cluster of circuit boards hanging from an exposed hatch on the side of the spacecraft's hull. 'That's the imaging circuit of a cloaking-shield generator, or at least it would be if it wasn't all banged up and broken and nibbled by sea bass. That's how they've kept it hidden all this time and why you've not seen it before now. But they've been unlucky, didn't bargain on the sea being so unpredictable. It's bashed the ship against the rocks, quite recently by the looks of things, hit a vital spot, probably invalidated their no claims bonus. Now, that's very unlucky for them, but very, *very* lucky for us, 'cause otherwise you'd never have found it.'

'But why?' Bronwyn was looking frightened. 'Why are they here?'

The Doctor nodded at the cables that clung to the walls. 'I think it's got something to do with the lighthouse. Come on! Let's go and see if I'm right!'

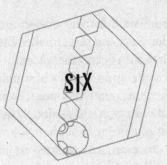

SIX

Rose had never been so glad to see the sky in her life. Using the torch that Ali had brought, the two of them had made swift progress through the tunnel, eventually reaching a large metal shutter bolted to the wall. It was rusted and corroded, but had been levered open with an old railway sleeper. By the two boys presumably. A shaft of weak sunlight sliced across the wet brickwork, rain spattering fitfully through the gap.

Rose looked at how far it had been prised open. It was going to be a tight squeeze to get through. Ali had wanted to go first, but Rose held her back, still not sure of what they were going to find on the other side.

Handing Ali the torch, she peered through the gap. The tunnel opened into a ramshackle lean-to in the corner of a sprawling courtyard. Packing crates, oil drums and the remains of an old sit-on lawnmower stopped her getting a better view. She pushed herself flat against the wall, forcing one shoulder through, then the other. Rust and dirt streaked the front of her parka but Rose didn't care, she was out.

Keeping low behind the piles of junk, she scurried forward, checking that the coast was clear. The courtyard was empty. It had obviously been stables for the rectory at one point, though now it was more like a junkyard. Once-ornate furniture lay in disregarded piles, the upholstery sodden and dirty. Paintings with broken frames and torn canvases were stacked against one wall, while a huge elegant dining table, its varnished surface streaked with scratches, was propped up in a corner. Presumably they had all been cleared out to make way for the beds and medical equipment that Morton had installed in the dining room.

On the other side of the courtyard was the house. Half a dozen tall, cylindrical metal bins were clustered together along the rear wall next to a winding fire escape. At some point Rose needed to take a look in those bins, but not with Ali around. God only knew what she was going to find inside.

Alongside the bins, almost at floor level, was a row of small, dirty windows. The cellar. Rose nodded. The two boys had said they'd been able to see into the cellar. That was where she would start.

'Rose!'

Ali was watching her from the tunnel, eyes wide.

Rose had hoped that common sense and more than a little fear would make the girl stay put in the safety of the shadows, but Ali seemed to be determined to join in the 'adventure'.

Rose beckoned her across and Ali darted over to where Rose was crouched. Rose caught her by the shoulders and looked her in the eyes.

'I need you to be very quiet now. You see those windows across there?' Rose pointed across the courtyard. 'I'm gonna go and have a look. Once I've done that, I'm gonna look in the bins and then we'll go back down the tunnel to find Billy and the others, OK?'

'OK.'

'Now I want you to stay hidden here.'

Ali opened her mouth to protest, but Rose raised a finger to her lips.

'I mean it, Ali. It's not a game. Stay here, all right?'

The little girl didn't look happy but she nodded nonetheless. Satisfied, Rose peered out into the courtyard again. It was still deserted.

'Well, now or never,' she muttered to herself.

Slipping out of the lean-to, Rose hurried across the courtyard, keeping to the wall, using the piles of furniture as cover. There was no movement from the house, no light from any of the windows. There wasn't even any birdsong. It was eerie.

A noise made her start and she ducked down behind a high-backed chair. A door opened and a white-coated figure emerged, carrying a bulging black refuse bag. The figure crossed to the bins and tossed the bag in, then hurried back inside the house.

As the door slammed shut Rose shot a look over at where Ali was hiding. She had tucked herself deep into the shadows of the lean-to. Rose waved at her to stay put.

One eye on the door, Rose darted across to the house, pressing up against the stone, making herself as small as possible. She ducked down, peering in through one of the narrow windows. The glass was filthy and she had to wipe at the dirt with her sleeve. She cupped her hands around her eyes, pressing her face against the glass.

The room she could see was large and low-ceilinged, lit by a single light bulb. Dozens of cardboard boxes piled high with books and ledgers were stacked against one wall, rolls of carpet underlay against another. A wine rack full of dusty bottles and spider's webs dominated a third wall and an old exercise bike was propped up in the far corner. It was like a million cellars in a million homes: boring, dull and ordinary. Rose felt a wave of disappointment. She'd hoped to be able to report back to the Doctor with proof that Morton was up to no good and, given what the boys had told her, she'd thought the cellar was her best bet.

She cursed under her breath. This was turning out to be a waste of time.

She was about to go to investigate the tall metal bins instead when something caught her eye in the shadows of the cellar. A bag tossed casually into a corner, half covered with an old tarpaulin. A long canvas bag, with fishing rods protruding from the open zip.

Rose's heart leapt into her mouth. Her dream. The fisherman. This was the proof that she'd been after, an indication that he *had* been down at the shore. She leaned her weight against the window frame, seeing if it would move. The catch inside flexed slightly but the frame held. She wasn't going to get in here.

She started to work her way along the wall of the house, pulling and pushing at each of the narrow windows in turn, oblivious now to the rain that had started to pour from the leaden sky. There! One of the catches was loose, the screws pulling from the rotten wood. She needed something to lever with.

Keeping low, she ducked over to the pile of furniture. Leaning against the back of one of the chairs was a roll of stair carpet. The house was quite old-fashioned. If she was lucky…

She pulled the chair to one side and allowed herself a smile of satisfaction. There. Stair rods. Perfect. Hefting one of them in her hands, she crossed back to the window. Slipping the stair rod through the narrow gap, she levered it back against the brickwork. The rod bent slightly, but she could feel the rotten woodwork starting to give… She readjusted her position, getting a better angle to push against the catch, and leaned all her weight on the stair rod.

There was a splintering crack and the window popped open, the catch pinging off. Rose stumbled forward, just catching the window before it swung closed again, wincing at the noise of the catch as it clattered on the flagstoned floor of the cellar. She shot a wary glance at the back door. Nothing.

Carefully she placed the stair rod on the floor and swung her leg through the open window, feeling with her toes for a firm foothold. With a quick glance back at the waiting Ali, who was watching her open-mouthed, she slipped through the gap and into the house.

The old iron padlock on the lighthouse door disintegrated into a thousand tiny fragments, literally shaken apart by the high-frequency sound waves from the Doctor's sonic screwdriver. The door itself was vibrating violently, rust and paint peeling off and whipping away in the wind.

Bronwyn had her hands clamped over her ears, trying to shut out the whine of the screwdriver and the deep throbbing hum that came from the door. The Doctor seemed oblivious to the noise, holding the little sonic device straight out in front of him, clearing years of corrosion in a matter of seconds.

With a flourish he finally turned it off and pushed at the door, which swung inwards, creaking alarmingly. He gave a satisfied smile and ducked through. A spiral metal staircase faced him, leading up the inside of the tower. He bounded up it, taking two steps at a time. Bronwyn followed him uncertainly, steadying herself on the less than secure handrail. Round the walls wound the same thick black cable that they had seen in the cave, snaking up through a neat hole drilled in the concrete of the floor, the alien technology harsh and new against the rusted metal of the old lighthouse. Bronwyn eyed it warily, as if it might uncoil from the wall and attack her at any moment.

The steps were slick with water and it took her several minutes to make her way up to the top of the tower, testing each step gingerly, pausing now and then to catch her breath. Rain lashed in through the broken windows and the wind swirled around her, flapping her oilskin.

She struggled on, emerging into the room where the lamp had once been housed. The machine that now sat there was certainly no light to warn off ships. It was a squat, black cylinder, its surface ridged and vented, dozens of tiny lights flickering across complex clusters of controls. The thick cable that snaked up the tower wound in and out of exposed sections of the machine like a worm through an apple core. The entire thing throbbed with malevolent power.

The Doctor was scurrying around it, prodding at sections with his sonic screwdriver, peering through vents, examining it from all angles. There was a look of satisfaction on his face and he flashed Bronwyn a dazzling smile.

'Knew that it had something to do with the lighthouse, just knew it! Isn't it gorgeous?'

'What is it?' Bronwyn didn't want to go anywhere near.

'Not entirely sure.'

The Doctor tapped his teeth with the handle of his sonic screwdriver, then pointed at a small panel.

'This bit's a behaviour inhibitor, usually used on farming planets to keep the livestock under control. Induces extreme anxiety if they stray too far from their fields. Probably why the locals are so reluctant to get anyone in to sort out their problems. Someone's gone to a lot of trouble to stop them calling for help.'

'You going to turn it off, then?'

'Ah, well, that might be a bit hasty. Whoever put this here did so because they can cover the entire village from this spot.'

The Doctor crouched down, peering through a grille.

'This is a wide-beam transmitter of some kind. Or receiver. But I'm not entirely sure what it does, and I hate to go around poking at things until I know what they do. Could cause untold damage. Besides, there's lots of power going in. Lots and lots of power.' He frowned. 'Ridiculous amounts of power, in fact. That little spacecraft must be working flat out when this thing is going at full tilt.'

'Is it safe? I mean, are we safe?'

'Oh yes.' The Doctor nodded vigorously. 'This thing's just on tick-over.' He tapped at a dial. 'No worries while the power is down at this level.'

There was a sharp click. Lights sprang to life all across the machine. The low hum started to rise in pitch.

'Ah,' said the Doctor.

Rose lowered herself gently on to the floor of the cellar, listening for any sign that her entrance into the house had been heard. She let the window swing shut gently and peered through the dusty gloom.

Distant muffled footsteps could be heard from overhead and there was the soft, low throb of machinery, generators of some kind, she supposed, but other than that it was silent. Rose crossed to the bag, pulling it out from under the tarpaulins. The fishing rods had been pushed in hurriedly without breaking them down properly, fishing line wound round everything in an untidy knot. Seeing the glint of fish hooks in the dim light from the bare bulb, Rose dragged the bag over to the window, determined to get a better look. Her fingers touched something sticky.

She held her hand up to the light and swallowed hard.
Dark red stains smeared her fingertips. Blood.

Grimacing, she wiped her fingers on the damp
canvas of the bag and opened the zipper carefully. It
was what you would expect of a bag packed for a
fishing trip: reels of line, cans of bait, carefully packed
sections of various styles of fishing rod. A peaked cap
and a stainless-steel Thermos flask were stuffed into a
wide pocket at one end and there was a scrap of paper,
an advert for holidays at Ynys Du.

Rose unfolded it, looking at the cheery sunlit
pictures of the harbour and the lighthouse. 'You'll
never want to leave,' read the cheery headline.

'Yeah. Right.'

Rose stuffed the advert back into the bag, zipped it
closed and dragged it back to where she had found it.
She needed more evidence than this. She needed
something that identified the man. It had been a vain
hope that Morton and his cronies would have left
anything that incriminating just lying about. She
looked around the cellar in frustration. There was
nothing.

The background hum of the generators suddenly
changed in pitch, deepening, the vibration setting the
wine bottles rattling in their frames. Rose frowned.
The noise was rhythmic and regular, almost like a
heartbeat; she could feel the vibrations deep in her
stomach. Another sound cut above the vibration, a

high-pitched chattering and beeping.

'That's not a generator,' Rose murmured.

On the far side of the cellar a set of steps led up to the only door. It was slightly ajar. Rose crossed to it, climbing the short set of stone steps and pressing her eye to the gap.

The door opened into a tall, vaulted corridor lined with pillars and arches. There was a dark wooden staircase against one end. The corridor was empty. Easing the door open, Rose slipped out. The cellars were more extensive than she had thought. Each arch led off to another room piled high with junk. Perhaps she would be lucky and find the evidence that she was looking for after all.

The noise of machinery was louder now, almost painful. It was coming from one of the arches at the far end of the corridor. Wincing, Rose edged her way forward. There was a harsh, pulsing glow from behind the pillars that sent long fingers of light flickering across the vaulted ceiling. She could see the outlines of tall, gleaming machines ranged against the cellar walls, bundles of cables fixed clumsily to the ancient brickwork.

She stepped down into the throbbing room in astonishment. It was full, packed floor to ceiling with technology. Tall silver cabinets were stacked against each wall, lights flickering deep inside them, while a large central console was bolted to the flagstones in the centre of the room. Cables and conduits snaked off into the shadows. Monitors showing the sleeping figures in the dining room hung in an ungainly tangle from the ceiling and huge power units throbbed in a corner.

It was like mission control from some space shot, and certainly not the product of anything on Earth. Rose shook her head in amazement. Not the evidence she had been looking for, but certainly something that the Doctor would want to know about.

She circled the console, trying to make sense of the flickering read-outs. Each set of controls seemed to relate to one of the sleeping figures upstairs. Heartbeat, respiration, brainwave activity.

'What the hell are you up to Morton?' she murmured.

The machinery suddenly shifted in pitch, the pulsing glow from the power units getting brighter, the vibrations stronger. Suddenly realising that she had been in the house longer than she had intended, Rose turned to make her way back out through the cellar window.

And stopped dead. At the bottom of the stairs was Miss Peyne, an unfriendly smile on her face, an ugly, snub-nosed pistol in her hand.

'Why, Miss Evans. You really have lost your way.'

Several of the lab-coated figures appeared at her shoulder. Rose was trapped.

* * *

The Doctor helped Bronwyn down the rickety spiral staircase, the noise from the machine in the lamp room humming in his ears. It had increased steadily over the last few minutes as more and more panels sprang to life across its surface.

'We're going already?' Bronwyn was not happy. 'After you've dragged me all the way up here? I wish you'd make up your mind!'

'Well, ideally I would have loved to stay and see what surprises the machine has in store, but there are dangerous amounts of power being fed through it. I have no idea what prolonged exposure to the transmissions might mean for either you or me, so better safe than sorry, eh? I suggest that we beat a hasty retreat, then collect up some of my equipment so that I can analyse what the machine was doing from a considerably safer distance.'

They emerged on to the rocks at the base of the lighthouse. The Doctor craned his neck, looking back up the tower. A pale, sickly glow from the lamp room now lit up the darkening sky. They had been on the island longer than he thought and night was rapidly sneaking up on them.

Bronwyn noticed it too and started back towards the cove where her boat was moored.

'We must go. We've been here too long.' The old woman sounded genuinely scared.

The Doctor nodded. 'I tend to agree.'

Catching hold of her arm to steady her, the Doctor guided Bronwyn over the wet rocks towards the shore. He could see her little boat bobbing animatedly in the surf, tethered to the large craggy outcrop.

Then suddenly there was an explosion of spray and something huge and dark burst from the ocean, its back ridged and barnacled. With a grating roar, it immediately vanished beneath the waves again.

Bronwyn gave a moan, wringing her hands. 'Too late. We've left it too late. It's always the same. Every night, as soon as the children start to go to sleep.'

The Doctor stared at her, open-mouthed. 'What did you say?' He slapped his hand against his forehead. 'I am a *total* bonehead... Every night... sleep... It's not the monsters! Those monsters don't create the nightmares. The nightmares create the monsters! And those transmitters in the machine, it's them. They're affecting the children... *causing* the nightmares!'

The Doctor stared out at the churning waves. 'And now...' he said. 'Now the children are going to sleep.' He watched as, all across the island, things started to emerge from the sea.

Rose had tried half-heartedly to make a break for it, but it had been a futile gesture. Two of the white-coated warders now held her by the arms. She struggled to shake herself loose, but they held her in a grip like steel.

'Ow. You're hurting me.'

Miss Peyne nodded and they relaxed their hold. Rose rubbed at her bruised arms, staring at the masked figures that surrounded her.

'All right. You don't have to keep up the surgeon act. I'm not contagious. There's no need for the masks.'

'Quite right, Miss Evans. I think we've worn all our masks quite long enough.'

Each of the warders reached up in unison, grabbing their surgical masks and peeling them back. There was a horrible wet sucking noise. Rose stepped back in shock. It wasn't just the masks that the warders peeled away, but their entire faces!

Miss Peyne gave a leering smile.

'Now, isn't that better?'

She grasped her own chin and pulled. Her entire face came away with the same wet sucking noise, revealing dark reptilian skin and gleaming malevolent eyes.

Miss Peyne and all the warders were aliens!

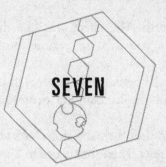

SEVEN

Rose stared in horrified fascination at the aliens that surrounded her. They were without doubt among the most unpleasant-looking creatures that she had come across.

Each of them was a dark green-grey colour, their skin wrinkled and ridged like decaying fruit. Short tufts of greasy hair sprouted from around a flattened, pug-like nose and their eyes were yellow slits, like a cat's. The mouths were wide and studded with sharp protruding teeth and a ridge of transparent spines ran over the tops of their heads, vanishing into the collars of their surgical gowns.

To Rose, Miss Peyne looked the most bizarre of all. From the neck down she was still the stick-thin, prissy woman who had greeted them at the door, her tweed jacket still buttoned neatly beneath her lab coat, her shoes still clean and polished. But the head was now slimy and lizard-like, a thin tongue flicking through yellowing teeth. The effect was like that children's game where you mix up various heads, legs and torsos.

The aliens jabbered to themselves in hissing tones, their human masks hanging grotesquely in their hands.

Miss Peyne shot them a vicious look and instructed them to be quiet. Then she turned to Rose, her mouth widening unpleasantly.

'Well, my dear, I'm impressed. You seem to be taking all this in your stride.'

Rose tried to sound more blasé than she felt.

'Well, you know. When you've seen one alien species that disguises itself as human, you've seen them all. You'd get on well with the Slitheen. You can trade fashion tips.'

'Ah, the dear Raxacoricofallapatorians. They do try so hard to integrate themselves seamlessly into society, but all that gas, it's so undignified.'

'Who are you?'

'Ah. Direct. Good.' The lizard tongue flickered out. 'We are the Cynrog. I am Peyne Tek Verlap, Priest Commander of the Third Cynrog Scientific Militia.'

'Miss Peyne.' Rose snorted. 'Very good. Very original.'

'An amusement. And an identity for the necessary dealings we have with your unpleasant species.'

'And what dealings would those be, eh?' Rose was

bolder now, looking Peyne full in the face. 'Kidnapping old people, drugging them up to the eyeballs. Does Morton know what you get up to in his cellar? Can't imagine he manages to get down here with his wheelchair and that. Don't think he'd be happy.'

The wide smile faded. 'You're quite right. Nathaniel does find it difficult to get down here, so we should be polite and pay him a visit, don't you think?'

Peyne gestured towards the stairs. 'After you, Miss Evans.'

Ali watched from the doorway to the cellar as Rose was ushered up the stairs by the grey-skinned monsters. Her heart was hammering in her chest. Monsters. Real monsters. Not like the ones from her nightmares, not like the ones that she drew night after night, but something far more tangible and terrifying. Monsters that hid under human masks!

Rose vanished through the door at the top of the stairs and the monster that had once been the frightening woman slammed it shut. Ali crept back down the stone steps and crouched at the bottom, leaning against the cool of the wall and wondering what to do next. She knew that she shouldn't have followed Rose, but in the end it had seemed that she didn't have much choice.

She had waited in the lean-to for what seemed like

for ever after Rose had vanished through the cellar window. Eventually she had decided that she would count to 100, then go and get the others.

The first 100 had come and gone. Then another, followed by another. The clouds had started to close in overhead and the sky had grown darker. Night was starting to fall and Ali was getting scared.

As the sky grew black and the rain became heavier she knew she had to make a decision. Either to go back down the tunnel and fetch the others or to find out what was happening to Rose. She peered down the tunnel, but now, in the fading light, it seemed far blacker than it had earlier. The little LEDs in her torch barely made an impression on the gloom.

Besides, Ali reasoned, if it was getting dark, then the monsters would start to roam the woods. It was always at dusk when you first started to hear them – the roars and howls. She hoped her friends had had the sense to leave before it got too dark.

Aware that she was probably going to be in big trouble when she got home, Ali had edged her way across the courtyard, eyes fixed on the narrow window that Rose had vanished through.

The window was heavy and it had taken all her strength to lift it. The smell of the cellar almost made her sneeze, it was so dusty and dank.

'Rose?' she'd whispered as loud as she dared. 'Are you there?'

Silence.

So, with a last look around the courtyard, Ali had taken a deep breath and slipped through into the dark cellar.

The floor was further down than she had realised and she'd nearly overbalanced as the window swung shut behind her. Teetering precariously on the window sill, she swung round, lowering herself down slowly until she touched the floor with the toe of her trainers.

The cellar was dark and empty, but Ali had heard noises coming from the door on the far side of the room, and voices. Sneaking over, she had peered through the gap into the corridor beyond, watching as a tall lady and several of the creepy masked nurses had surrounded Rose.

Then had come the part that nearly made Ali scream, the part where they had ripped their faces off, revealing the horrible monsters underneath. She had wanted to run and hide, but she knew that if she made the slightest noise the monsters would capture her too.

Now she waited in the dark, waited until she was certain that they had all gone, then slipped through into the corridor once again. The noise from the strange machinery was giving her a headache, so she stuck her fingers in her ears. Slowly she made her way towards the door at the top of the stairs. Holding her breath, she reached out and turned the handle. It wasn't locked and the door swung open.

Ali paused for a moment. This was the point of no return. She thought about the tunnel and the wood full of monsters that she would have to go through if she tried to go back. Then she thought of Rose, alone and in the clutches of these new monsters. Rose was her friend. She couldn't leave without trying to help.

With a deep breath, Ali stepped through the doorway and into the house.

The Doctor and Bronwyn huddled at the base of the lighthouse, their backs pressed against the wet steel trying desperately not to attract the attention of the hulking monstrosity that snuffled and scraped at the ground on the other side.

The falling of night had been like a signal for the creatures to appear. All across the island they had swarmed out of the sea, slithering and crawling over the rocks. Something huge had swept above the lighthouse on leathery wings earlier. The Doctor still hadn't managed to get a good look at that particular monster, though perhaps this was a good thing.

The two of them had headed away from the coast and back towards the lighthouse. Bronwyn had pleaded with the Doctor to try and make it to the boat. Surely they would be safe out at sea? The Doctor had refused. Once they were out on the open ocean, they would be trapped, easy prey for any of the creatures that could swim or fly. No. They needed room to manoeuvre, not to mention time for him to formulate some kind of plan.

The sickly glow from the lighthouse and last remnants of the dying sun had afforded them glimpses of the things that now prowled across Black Island. Some crawled on squat legs, others writhed on tentacles. Spider shapes and dinosaur shapes mixed with strange combinations of scales, feathers and fur. The creatures truly did come from the imagination of children; they conformed to no known process of evolution. Limbs and bodies had been thrust together with imaginative abandon, the colours of their hides drawn from the palette of a nursery-school painting set.

Not that it made them any less dangerous. Each of the shambling horrors was equipped with a fearsome armoury of fangs and claws. The Doctor had watched as just one of the monsters had cut a bloody swathe through the colony of seals, wiping out dozens of them with each swipe of a razor-sharp claw.

He had had to stop Bronwyn from rushing forward to try and save them. Instead, he had dragged the old woman away. And now they were trapped here, back at the lighthouse, hiding in the shadows, desperately trying to stay out of sight as the monsters spread out across the island.

The fact that the creatures had appeared within moments of the machine in the lighthouse springing to life had connected two more pieces of the puzzle and the Doctor had started to formulate some very nasty theories. He badly needed to examine the machine more closely, disable it if at all possible, but when they had arrived at the lighthouse they found the doorway blocked by a shambling, lank-haired beast with huge tusks, gnawing on the remains of one of the unfortunate seals.

Keeping to the scrubby gorse bushes and darting from boulder to boulder, they had managed to make it around to the far side of the lighthouse. Now the Doctor was just waiting for the right time to make a dash for the doorway.

He peered around the base of the lighthouse. The creature had its back to him, concentrating on its meal. A thick tail, studded with wicked spikes, thrashed aimlessly. There was no chance of getting past that without being torn to pieces. The rest of the monsters were concentrated over by the decimated seal colony, feasting on the corpses that littered the rocks.

'What are we going to do?' Bronwyn's voice was trembling. 'The things are everywhere.'

'If we can just get back inside the lighthouse I can lock us in.' The Doctor brandished his sonic screwdriver. 'It won't take long. We just need a few seconds to get through the door.'

'We'll never make it with that thing in the way.'

'We need a distraction, that's all.' The Doctor took another peek around the lighthouse. 'And I think one is just arriving.'

The distraction came in the form of another of the beasts from the children's nightmares. Gorged on seal, a spindly spider-like creature clattered towards them, mandibles dripping with gore. The thing blocking their way to the lighthouse gave a low grumbling roar, its tail smashing down on the rocks. With an ear-splitting screech, the spider thing launched itself forward and the two monsters crashed together, tumbling end over end down the slope towards the thunderous surf.

Seizing the moment, the Doctor caught hold of Bronwyn's hand, hauling her up and dragging her around the doorway. He bundled her inside the lighthouse, heaving the heavy steel door shut with his shoulder. Leaning all his weight against it, he fumbled for his sonic screwdriver. It sprang to life with a keening buzz, the blue light at its tip fusing the metal of the door to its frame.

The Doctor worked at it for a few seconds, then stood back with a satisfied grin.

'That should hold 'em.'

As if on cue, something huge slammed against the door, shaking the whole lighthouse. The Doctor jumped backwards.

'Well, I *think* it'll hold them. For a while. Well, a bit of a while.'

Bronwyn gave him a hard stare. 'So have you locked them out or us in?'

'Let's just hope they don't like canned food, eh?' said the Doctor.

Morton's office in the old rectory was dark and quiet. In the centre of the room sat Morton in his wheelchair, fingers steepled and pressed to his lips, his eyes closed.

A fire cracked in the large old-fashioned grate and the music of Elgar drifted across from an old-fashioned record player: the last bars of his cello concerto. As the last note faded, a high screeching roar came from outside as something huge and monstrous lumbered past the house.

Morton opened his eyes and smiled. He wheeled himself over to the desk, picking up a heavy framed photograph. The picture was himself as a young man leaning on a cricket bat. The picture had been taken on the lawn out front many, many summers ago. Morton sighed. He had been through so much since then. So much pain and torment. But soon, soon it would all be finished.

The heavy door to his office swung open, shattering his peace, and Peyne pushed Rose roughly into the room. Morton swung around in his wheelchair, a frown furrowing his brow. He didn't like people entering his office unannounced. His frown turned to surprise.

'Miss Evans? And Miss Peyne.' He gave the alien a puzzled glance. 'You've slipped into something more comfortable, I see. I hope there is an explanation for this.'

Peyne crossed to his side. 'I found her in the power room,' she hissed.

'Really?' Morton looked up at Rose curiously. 'You really are very persistent, Miss…' He cocked his head to one side, looking at her expectantly.

Rose shuffled uncomfortably. 'Evans, I told you.'

'Oh yes? That's hardly original, even in Wales. There really is no point in lying to me any longer. You might as well just tell me the truth. It will make things so much easier in the long run.'

Rose shivered. She had the feeling that he wasn't bluffing. 'Tyler. It's Rose Tyler.'

'Better. And Dr… Jones? Is he around somewhere too? Do I need to send my people to flush him out?'

Rose shook her head. 'No, he's not here. But he knows where I am. If I'm not back soon he'll come and…'

'What?' Morton smiled. 'Come and pay your bail? Come and explain to the police what you were doing, trying to gain access to my affairs under an assumed name. Come and listen to you explaining why you were caught breaking and entering. Come and offer compensation for the criminal damage that you have no doubt caused gaining entry to my property.' He tutted condescendingly. 'No, no, no. I'm afraid that, if I want, you can be in an awful lot of trouble, young lady.'

'And what are you going to do about them?' Rose nodded at the Cynrog that lurked in the open doorway. 'How you gonna explain to the police that you've got alien nurses looking after your patients?'

Morton gave Peyne a look of surprise. 'She *is* well informed. How refreshing. Perhaps the police aren't such a good idea after all.'

'Oh, I dunno,' said Rose. 'Bring 'em on. I'm sure they'd be interested in hearing about you covering up that death on the beach.'

Morton stiffened in his chair and his tone changed. 'It seems that you have been digging rather deeper into my affairs than I had realised. Perhaps we do need to tighten up our operation a little. Peyne, whatever it is she found get rid of it. Then make sure that she was alone. Get your men to make a thorough sweep of the grounds. And tell them to put their masks back on. We don't want any prying eyes seeing too much, do we?'

Peyne gestured to her unmasked colleagues and they snapped to attention, pulling the surgical masks with their human faces back into place and hurrying away down the corridor.

Rose nodded after them. 'Couldn't afford proper masks for that lot, then? Had to resort to cheap fancy-dress nurses' outfits for everyone except matron here?'

'Quite so.' Morton wheeled himself over to her. 'Full lip synch in the masks is very expensive to achieve and I'm afraid the Cynrog are sticklers for working to an exact budget. Miss Peyne here is the only one who needs direct interaction with the populace. The others are merely disguised for the benefit of nosy, interfering busybodies.'

'So what are you up to, Morton? What deal have you done with the Cynrog? Running a nursing home for them?'

'You know nothing.' Morton's voice was low and measured.

'Those things are killing people, Morton!' Rose was getting angry now, frustrated by the calmness of the man in front of her. 'Does she tell you about her little night-time trips to clean up the mess that's left when your monsters have finished eating? Does she? People are going to be missed. You can't just keep on with what you're doing without someone noticing!'

Morton wheeled himself slowly over to the desk. He opened a drawer and pulled out a plastic bag. Inside Rose could see a wallet, some credit cards and a set of car keys. Morton unsealed the bag and pulled out a driver's licence. He studied it sadly for a moment. Then held it up for Rose to see.

'Carl Jenkins. Twenty-eight years old. No parents, and a sister who is currently serving time at Her Majesty's Pleasure for aggravated assault.' He gave Rose a sad smile. 'Do you really think that anyone is going to miss him? His death was unfortunate, but the simple truth is that the world will never notice his passing. He is simply irrelevant.'

He tossed the driving licence on to the fire, watching the plastic curl and smoulder.

'The work we are doing here cannot be interrupted. If death is the price that has to be paid, then so be it. Sacrifices must be made.' He sealed the bag again and handed it to Peyne. 'Dispose of that in the incinerator. No traces.'

Rose felt a cold fury towards this man who regarded life so casually.

'Whatever it is you're doing the Doctor will stop you. Harm those kids and I'll stop you.'

'You know nothing!' Morton repeated, this time slamming the palms of his hands down on the arms of his wheelchair, his calm demeanour gone. 'You have no idea of what I have had to endure! Of what I have gone through to get to this point! I am not the child-murdering monster that you take me for. You can't even begin to understand!' He stopped, his face dangerously red, and slowly tried to control his harsh breathing. 'Peyne, I want to know who she is and where she comes from.'

Peyne smiled unpleasantly. 'Certainly, Nathaniel.'

'And I want to know quickly. Use the machine.'

The smile faded. 'But we have just started the night's operations. If we interrupt the sequence…'

'An hour's delay will not matter!' snapped Morton. 'The night is still young. I need to know if there is any danger of delay to our plans. I need to know who she is and who this mysterious Doctor of hers is. Or would you prefer to explain to your Grand Synod that you had advance intelligence and failed to act on it?'

Peyne said nothing, but her eyes were full of hate.

'Then do as I say!'

Peyne glowered at him before turning and pulling an old-fashioned bell pull in the corner of the room. Morton took a handkerchief from his pocket and mopped his brow.

'Now, Miss Tyler, we shall really get to the bottom of things.'

Two of the masked warders appeared in the doorway.

'Prepare a bed for our guest.'

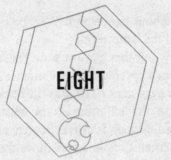

EIGHT

The Doctor lay flat on his back, peering into the guts of the alien machine, his sonic screwdriver acting as a torch.

The pale green glow cast by the machinery crackled around him, sending sparks of energy across the fibres of his jacket like St Elmo's fire. The Doctor glanced down at his glittering jacket warily. There was an enormous amount of power being generated by this machine, a lot of it that he still didn't understand. The readings he had taken indicated that it was safe, at least for a short time, but he didn't want to be exposed to it any longer than was absolutely necessary.

Bronwyn was perched on the stairs just outside the doorway of the lamp room. She'd refused to stay at the base of the lighthouse, and the Doctor couldn't really say that he blamed her – the noise of the monsters' claws scraping along the steel plating was enough to give anyone nightmares – but he was concerned about exposing her to the unquantifiable radiation of the lamp room.

There was another reason too. The machine was operating on a psychic level in some way. The Doctor could feel a persistent tickling at the back of his mind. Its effect on the children of the village was now obvious; its effect on him was merely an irritation – his own mental discipline was more than enough to keep the intrusion of the machine at bay – but Bronwyn was another story. Her mental state was in a very delicate balance already and the Doctor couldn't say what effect the machine might have on her.

'Assuming it hasn't had an effect on you already,' the Doctor muttered.

'What was that?' Bronwyn frowned at him. 'You'll have to speak up.'

'Nothing. I'm still trying to formulate some kind of plan, that's all.'

'Well, we can't stay in the lighthouse for ever.'

'We're hardly likely to make it back to the shore in one piece either!'

The Doctor could imagine what aquatic horrors lurked in the waters around Black Island.

'What are we going to do, then?' Bronwyn asked, wincing as the lighthouse reverberated with another attack from the creatures outside.

'I think our best bet at the moment is to try and get to the cave and its mysterious spacecraft. There's a possibility that I can open the main hatch and we can shelter in there. I doubt that even these creations of nightmare could break into a duralinium hull.'

Bronwyn snorted. 'How are you going to get into an alien spacecraft?'

'I'm quite good with locks.' The Doctor gave her an apologetic smile. 'Look, Bronwyn, I'm trying to concentrate. Please?'

He stretched his neck with a view to squeezing himself further underneath the machine. He was determined to get a closer look at the mechanisms. It wasn't easy, though. The machine was huge and heavy, bolted to the floor of the lamp room with massive, blind-headed nuts. The base was only thirty centimetres or so off the floor and pipes wound through every available space. The Doctor peered through the tangle.

'Aha!'

Six ugly metal lumps studded a curving section of the machine's underside.

'*That's* how you affected Rose's dreams in the TARDIS!' The Doctor shifted his position, trying to get a closer look. 'The machine has telepathic aerials of some kind. Not only is it sending out transmissions that affect the children's dreams, but it's also acting as a receiver, storing those dreams, utilising them in some way.'

The TARDIS had its own telepathic circuits – that

was how it translated languages for him and Rose whenever they landed on an alien world. It must have picked up transmissions from the machine when they materialised to take bearings, meaning that Rose's dream had been influenced in the same way as the dreams of the children in the village. The Doctor's mind was racing, piecing the puzzle together.

'The machine must be tapping directly into the psychic reservoir of the children's nightmares, manipulating them in some way and then taking images *from* those nightmares and generating them as physical entities. But why? Who would want to populate Wales with creatures from children's nightmares?'

One thing was certain. He had been right that this machine was the key to everything that was going on. If he could just disengage the telepathic circuits then the machine would no longer function.

'Disable the machine's telepathic ability, stop the monsters. Easy.'

The Doctor stretched again, trying to reach the cluster of metal protuberances. His fingers brushed the side of one of them, but the space between floor and machine was too tight for him to reach.

'Then again, perhaps it's *not* going to be that easy.'

He sat back upright, studying the panels of lights and switches that littered the surface of the machine. The equipment was complicated even by his standards and starting to mess randomly with the controls might have dire consequences for the children being affected.

'What are you doing under there?' asked Bronwyn, peering through the door.

'Thinking!'

His only option seemed to be to unbolt the machine from the floor in order to reach the telepathic generators, and that was going to take time. He sighed.

'I hope you didn't have any other plans for the evening.'

He started to shrug off his coat when there was a terrifying screech from behind him and the flap of leathery wings. Something sharp hit him in the small of the back, sending him sprawling, his sonic screwdriver clattering into a corner. He scrabbled across the floor to get it, but a huge talon slashed at his feet, sending him tumbling to the floor again.

Looming outside the lamp room was a huge pterodactyl-like creature, wings beating furiously as it scrabbled to gain a purchase on the wet steel of the lighthouse. The Doctor could see his face reflected in its beady black eyes. The creature threw its head back and screamed, before lunging at him with its razor-sharp beak.

Rose tried hard not to panic as the masked warders strapped her down to the metal-framed bed. Around her in the converted dining room the six sleeping figures lay still, their breathing slow and steady, the noise of the machines soft and rhythmic. Other warders sat at a bank of consoles along one wall, their hands moving in complex patterns over flickering controls, their eyes fixed on dozens of tiny read-outs.

Morton wheeled himself to Rose's side.

'You'll find it less unpleasant if you don't try to resist the machinery.'

Peyne crossed to his side, a complex arrangement of metal straps and coloured wires in her hands. It was some kind of helmet, a thick bundle of cables coiling across the floor to where two of the warders were setting up a console with a large screen attached to it.

Peyne lifted Rose's head from the pillow, jamming on the helmet. Rose winced as it tugged at her hair.

'Careful, Miss Peyne.' Morton's voice was mocking. 'We don't want to damage that pretty head. Not before it's told us what we want to know.'

'And then what?' Rose strained to pull against the straps. 'Another accident on the beach with one of your monsters?'

'That depends.'

'On what?'

'On whether you have a mind that is useful to our plans or not.'

Morton glanced up at Peyne, who was adjusting controls on the console now.

'How long?'

'We have to calibrate the machine. A few minutes.'

Morton patted Rose's arm. 'We won't keep you waiting long.'

The Doctor tore himself free from the grasping claws of the flying monster, scrambling around to the other side of the lamp room as the creature's beak slammed into the floor. Hissing in anger, it thrust its long scrawny neck in further through the window, claws scrabbling. Snatching his coat up from the floor, the Doctor used it to beat at the head of the monster, sending it flapping off into the night screaming.

He watched as it wheeled against the boiling clouds before turning and sweeping back down again, slamming into the lighthouse and renewing its attack with fury. The Doctor dodged to one side as the beak snapped next to his head with a loud kklak! He darted around the machine once more, trying to keep it between him and the screeching thing. The creature had positioned itself in the window directly above the stairwell, so there was no way he could get there without coming in range of that wickedly sharp beak.

The Doctor craned his neck over the edge, desperately looking for a way to escape. The shrieking cries were starting to attract the other creatures and slowly, one by one, they were all converging on the lighthouse.

'Doctor?' Bronwyn's voice was terrified. 'Doctor? What's happening? What's that noise?'

The pterodactyl thing cocked its head to one side, its cold eyes fixed on the top of the stairs.

Before the Doctor could shout any warning, Bronwyn's head appeared again, peering cautiously into the lamp room. The creature pulled its own head back to strike, screaming in triumph.

'No!'

The Doctor hurled himself forward, fists clenched, determined that these things would not claim another victim.

His fists met only open air. Bronwyn took a step back in shock, almost tripping and tumbling down the spiralling stairs.

'What on earth are you doing?' she screamed.

The Doctor looked around in amazement. The pterodactyl thing had gone. The glow from the alien machine had faded too, the controls on its surface now silent and dark. Cautiously, the Doctor peered out of the shattered window. Far below, the island was quiet and empty, the only sound that of surf crashing against the rocks and the soft hiss of rain.

The Doctor turned to the bewildered Bronwyn. 'They've gone,' he said. 'They've all gone!'

Morton and Peyne were hunched over the control console, peering intently at the small display screen.

Behind them Rose was writhing on the bed, straining against the straps, her eyes closed, a frown of pain flickering across her brow.

'The machine is recalibrated for her gender and age,' Peyne said, adjusting a control. 'We can begin.' Her finger hovered over a pulsing button.

Morton nodded and Peyne stabbed her finger down.

Rose knew that she was dreaming again. It was like before, a sense of hovering over her shoulder, of being able to observe herself. But this time her dreams were not hers; this time she knew that others were manipulating her thoughts, driving her dreams in a direction they had determined. She desperately wanted to force herself to wake up, but the drugs wouldn't let her.

She could feel fingers in her mind, rummaging through her thoughts and memories. Slowly, things that she would rather have kept buried were being dredged to the surface.

'Fascinating!' Morton cried, leaning forward eagerly as shapes started to form on the small screen in front of him. 'Go deeper, Peyne. There is obviously far more to Miss Tyler and her mysterious friend than we at first thought.'

The Doctor stepped out of the lighthouse door and

looked around cautiously. Satisfied that there was no danger, he beckoned to Bronwyn to come and join him.

She scurried timidly to his side. 'Where did they all go?'

'I don't know, and at this particular moment in time I really don't care! That was one creepy-crawly too many for me and I think it's high time our little day trip came to an end, don't you?'

Bronwyn nodded vigorously.

'Right. Well, let's get back to your boat while we've got a chance.'

'You don't think they're going to come back?'

The Doctor looked up at the lamp room, which was now dark and dead. The monsters were linked to the machine and someone had turned that machine off. Whether by accident or design, it gave them an opportunity to get back to the mainland. He had no way of knowing how long it would be before the machine started working again and dismantling it at night would be virtually impossible. He needed to come back during the day, when his tinkering would have less chance of damaging side effects, he could actually see what he was doing and he had a better chance of not being eaten.

He patted Bronwyn on the shoulder. 'I think we should make the best of opportunities when they present themselves.'

The two of them started to make their way down the sloping rocks to where the boat was moored, the Doctor trying to manoeuvre Bronwyn away from the dozens of seal carcasses that lay like broken toys all around.

They reached the cove and Bronwyn hurried down to catch hold of the prow of the little motorboat. Fortunately, the monsters had ignored it – the seals had been a far more appetising target. The Doctor crossed to where the rope was tied. It was heavy with sea water and he struggled to undo the damp knot. It was nearly loose when there was a little cry of fear from the shoreline.

The Doctor looked up sharply. Bronwyn was holding a hand to her mouth in horror, staring into a rock pool. A dull orange glow illuminated her terrified face.

The Doctor bounded to her side. Bronwyn pointed in disbelief at a rock pool at the water's edge. The water had turned thick and treacly, glowing from within like lava. It then boiled and writhed like a living thing as a crude face formed on the surface.

'Time Lord!' The voice boomed around the island.

The Doctor stared incredulously at it. 'Impossible.'

'Doctor, look!'

Bronwyn tugged at his sleeve. Silhouetted against the sky, two large figures lumbered into view, pot-bellied and thick-legged, their huge clawed arms steadying them on the uneven surface. Jet-black eyes fixed on the Doctor and Bronwyn, and the things giggled horribly, like huge babies.

From somewhere in the dark there was a harsh grating cry: 'Seek! Locate! Exterminate!'

The Doctor turned and bundled Bronwyn towards the boat.

'Get it started! Now!'

Flustered, Bronwyn scrambled across the weed-slick rocks, hauling herself into the boat and fumbling with the starter cord of the engine. The Doctor unwound the rope from where it was tied, tossing it to Bronwyn and then hopping onboard himself.

The engine coughed and spluttered. For a moment the Doctor thought it was going to die, but then with a roar it caught, billowing bluish smoke around them. Bronwyn swung the handle of the outboard hard about and the motorboat swung in a tight circle. The prow lined up with the entrance to the cove and the boat surged forward, waves splashing across its prow.

The Doctor looked back at the island, eyes flicking from rock to rock desperately, hoping that they'd not left their escape too late. His eyes narrowed. A small figure stood on a craggy promontory watching them. Not a monster, but a small child. A boy clutching a ragged cloth toy.

As he watched, the child gave them a wave, then turned and vanished from view.

The Doctor's mind raced. Up to now the creatures that had stalked the woods and the island had been impossible imaginary creatures, their shapes and sizes drawn directly from the over-active imaginations of frightened children. The last few apparitions they had seen, however, had been quite different. The Nestene Consciousness, the Slitheen and the Daleks were all creatures that no earthbound child could possibly know about. They were creatures with their basis in fact, and here and now there was only one common denominator other than himself.

Rose.

NINE

Ali watched from her hiding place in a cupboard under the stairs as Rose was half-led, half-carried from the ward by two nurses. She ducked back out of sight, closing the cupboard door to a crack as they manoeuvred Rose across the hall and dragged her up the stairs. Their heavy footsteps sent trickles of dust down on where Ali had tucked herself between old Hoovers and boxes full of empty wine bottles. She covered her nose, determined not to sneeze.

Following Rose and her captors through the dark of the old rectory had been the most terrifying thing that Ali had ever done in her life. Every corner she rounded was a step into the unknown, every shadow was thick with menace. She had hurried up the stairs from the cellar, desperate not to lose sight of Rose, padding along darkened corridors, following the sound of footsteps echoing through the dusty old house.

She had nearly been caught as she made her way into

the wide hallway. A door had opened behind her and she had run forward blindly, expecting to be seen at any moment. But she had been lucky – the nurses in the hallway had their backs to her. She had spotted a cupboard under the stairs and dived into it, holding her breath as two more nurses rounded the corner, making their way across the hall and vanishing through two big double doors.

Ali had waited in the cool dark of the cupboard, watching as Rose was marched across the hall and pushed through those double doors by the woman with the gun. That had been ages ago. Ali had been wondering how long she would have to wait before trying to make her escape from the house when the doors had opened again and Rose had been dragged out.

Ali waited as short a time as she dared, then eased the cupboard door open again. The hallway was empty, all the doors closed. She could hear muffled voices from inside the old dining room.

Keeping one eye on the doors, she made her way carefully up the stairs, making as little sound as possible on the polished wood. She crept to the first landing, peering through the banisters to see where the nurses were taking Rose.

At the end of the corridor she could see one of them fumbling with a key in the lock of a big wooden door; the other one had Rose in his arms, keeping her upright. Ali scampered up the last few stairs, tucking herself behind a large wooden chest that stood on the landing. The nurse swung the door open and helped his colleague carry Rose inside, then they both emerged, locking the door and heading back towards the stairs.

Ali crouched down behind the chest, making herself as small as possible. She screwed her eyes up, listening as the footsteps came closer and closer. With a sigh of relief she heard them carry on past her, clunking down the stairs and echoing across the empty hallway.

She peered out from behind the chest. The hallway seemed deserted. Rain was streaming down the panes of a tall window at the end of the landing, sending flickering, writhing patterns over the walls and floor. Ali scampered across to the room where they had put Rose, keeping as close to the wall as possible. The big heavy key was still in the lock.

Ali reached out and turned it. The lock opened with a loud clunk. Terrified of being locked in once she was inside, she pulled the key out of the keyhole and slipped it into the pocket of her jeans. Checking that no one was coming down the corridor behind her, she then turned the big brass knob and heaved against the door.

It creaked alarmingly. Ali opened it just enough for her to slip through, then carefully closed it again. The room was dark and smelt musty. Heavy curtains covered the windows and huge ancient-looking wardrobes loomed over her. On the far side of the room she could see a bed with an unconscious figure draped across it awkwardly. It looked as though the nurses had just dumped Rose and left her. Ali scurried over to her side.

Rose looked dreadful. Her skin was pale and waxy and her hair tangled and matted. Her eyes were flickering left and right under her lids.

Ali grasped hold of her arm and shook it gently. 'Rose!' she hissed. 'Wake up!'

Rose's eyes cracked open, rolling unpleasantly as she made a great effort to focus. She tried to speak, but managed only a croaking gasp. Ali glanced around the room. There was a sink against one wall, one of those tiny old-fashioned types like her gran used to have in her upstairs bedroom. Ali crossed to it. A cracked glass sat on a little shelf below a grimy mirror. She stretched up and lifted it down, then grimaced. It was a bit grubby, full of dust and a dead spider. She reached in her pocket for a tissue. That was a bit grubby too, but it was all she had.

She shook the spider from the glass, wiped off as much of the dust as she could and turned on the cold tap. Pipes squealed and banged in protest at years of disuse, sounding impossibly loud in the dark room. Ali jumped. Then, with a coughing splutter, a trickle of cold water splashed into the basin. She rinsed the glass, filled it to the brim and soaked the tissue, then hurried back to Rose.

Hauling her upright, Ali pressed the cold tissue to Rose's forehead, brushing her hair back and wiping some of the sweat away.

'Here, I brought you some water.'

With unsteady hands, Rose took the glass and began swallowing down greedy gulps. Water splashed over her chin and on to the bed and she started to cough.

Ali snatched the glass from her. 'Slowly, or you're going to choke, stupid!'

Rose nodded weakly. 'Thanks,' she croaked. 'Great bedside manner.'

Ali gave her the glass back and Rose sipped at it more slowly.

'What are you doing here, Ali? I thought I told you to wait for me.'

'I was scared.' Ali looked at her feet guiltily. 'It started to get dark and they come out when it gets dark. The monsters.'

'So you followed me in here?'

Ali nodded. 'But the monsters are in here too. I saw them, when they took their faces off.' Ali could feel tears starting to well in her eyes, but she brushed them away angrily. 'Why are they here? Why did the monsters have to pick on our village?'

'Hey, it's OK.' Rose caught her by the hand, sitting her down on the edge of the bed and putting a comforting arm around her shoulders. 'You remember that friend of mine, the Doctor?'

Ali nodded.

'Well, he's an expert on monsters. Sorts 'em out all the time.'

'Really?'

'Really. He gives *them* nightmares.'

Ali managed a weak smile at the idea.

Rose eased herself cautiously to her feet, steadying herself on Ali's shoulder. Colour was slowly starting to come back to her face. She looked round the darkened room.

'Where are we?'

'They locked you in one of the bedrooms.' Ali held the key out proudly. 'But I got the key!' She looked at Rose quizzically. 'What were they doing to you? I saw them attach those wires and things to your head, but then they shut the door and I couldn't see any more.'

'I'm not sure. At first I thought they just wanted to find out who I was, but now I think maybe they were looking for something.'

'In your head?' Ali's eyes were wide. 'What did they want from inside your head?'

'I don't know.' Rose shook her head. 'I just don't know.'

Morton watched impatiently as Peyne flitted from console to console in the ward, adjusting controls, studying read-outs, making notes on a clipboard.

'Well? Is she any use to us or not?'

Peyne glowered at him, teeth bared from beneath her thin lips. 'No, Morton. As I thought, she is too old to be of use as an imager. Like most on this miserable planet, her mind is too tainted by the trivia of the real world, her thoughts too consumed with the confusion of life.'

'But the creatures.' Morton pointed at the screen. 'You saw them. Magnificent creations! Those things were not the product of an imagination obsessed with trivia!'

'Frankly, those creatures were not the product of imagination at all, Morton,' Peyne snapped. 'They were real-life experiences. Memories, not fantasy.'

'What?' Morton was shocked. 'How is that possible?'

Peyne smiled at him unpleasantly, greatly enjoying her moment of superiority. 'The girl is an inter-dimensional traveller. Her body is soaked with energy from the time winds. She appears to have a telepathic link with a machine called the TARDIS, one of the legendary time capsules of the Time Lords.'

'The Doctor...'

'Would appear to be one of those Time Lords.'

Peyne adjusted a control, bringing a flickering image of the Doctor to life on one of the dozens of screens.

'It's interesting. They are meant to be extinct, casualties of the war they started.' She ran a hand across the screen. 'I wonder where this one has been hiding.'

'Damn.' Morton wheeled himself angrily across the room. 'I'm not interested in your extinct Time Lords! Switch the machines back on! We've wasted enough time!'

'As I recall, it was your decision to turn them off in the first place.'

'All right, Peyne! It was my fault. I'm sure you will make sure that the Synod knows that you had nothing to do with it!'

Peyne nodded. 'My report will have to be submitted.' She crossed to the bank of machines again, flicking at switches. 'But before you dismiss the Doctor completely, consider this. The Time Lords are recorded as having the gift of complete bodily renewal. A useful attribute, don't you think?'

Morton stared at her silently and, with a smile, Peyne resumed her work at the controls.

Bronwyn's motorboat bumped hard against the harbour wall, engine roaring as she swung it hard into the side. The Doctor bounded out and swiftly climbed the rusty ladder that clung to the wall. Bronwyn clambered up clumsily after him, skirts held in one hand and the rope coiled untidily over her shoulder.

The Doctor helped her up on to the quay, watching impatiently as she carefully tied the boat to one of the bollards that studded the wall's edge. The harbour was deserted, the harbour master's office with its picture-postcard displays shuttered and dark. The place was like a ghost town again, the wind sending abandoned newspaper pages fluttering down the street like mad origami seagulls.

The windows of the pub were ablaze with light. The locals were no doubt all gathered inside once more, awaiting their nightly siege. Out in the bay, the green light was already starting to glow at the top of the lighthouse again.

The Doctor started off along the quay.

'Come on, Bronwyn! No dawdling! We've got to try and get up to the rectory before the woods start crawling with nasty things again. Chop-chop!'

The old lady shook her head. 'Goin' home.'

'What?' The Doctor hurried back to her. 'We've got to get up to Morton's place. Rose is in trouble.'

Bronwyn shook her head again and there was real fear in her eyes. The Doctor put an arm around her shoulder.

'I can't leave you out here alone. It's not safe.'

Bronwyn shook herself free angrily.

'It should be safe! A woman shouldn't feel frightened in the place she grew up in. We shouldn't have to hide.'

Torn, the Doctor watched her hobble her way along the harbour wall. Every second he delayed gave him less chance of reaching the rectory and helping Rose out of whatever it was she'd got herself into, but he couldn't leave Bronwyn out in the dark on her own. He called after her, but she didn't look back. So, with a sigh, he turned and hurried after her.

She was heading for the strip of beach and her ramshackle house. 'Told him not to come back.' She waved an angry finger at the Doctor. 'Told him that no good would ever come of it and now look where he's led us!'

Bronwyn's voice was getting louder and louder the angrier she got. She was going to wake up all the children if she carried on like this! The Doctor was about to say something but suddenly he stopped dead in his tracks.

'Of course!' He ran a hand through his tousled hair. 'That's it!'

He dashed forward, catching Bronwyn by the arm and spinning her around. 'Bronwyn Ceredig, you are a genius. A grade-A certified genius!' He planted a kiss on her forehead.

'What has got into you?' She slapped him away. 'Are you mad?'

'Completely! Totally! Mad as a hatter! Come on.' He caught her hand, steering her back towards the pub. 'I'm going to buy you a crème de menthe!'

Beth Hardy wiped tears from her eyes and glanced over at the door for what seemed like the millionth time. The mood in the pub was sombre and oppressive. On the other side of the bar Margo Evans was trying to comfort her two girls, while Jeff Palmer stood with his arm protectively around his son, Billy. Mervyn stood in the window with a face like thunder; he and Jeff had nearly come to blows.

It had been nearly two hours since Billy and the two girls had slunk nervously into the kitchen of the pub. They had been wet and splattered with mud, but there was nothing unusual in that. Beth had tutted at them sternly and berated them for trailing muck across her nice clean floor, waiting for Ali's mischievous face to poke around the edge of the doorframe at any moment.

Then Sian Evans had started to cry, and with a sudden cold chill Beth had realised that something was wrong.

They had managed to coax the story out of the three kids – Baz Morgan was already safely at home with his parents. Billy had told them about their meeting with Rose in the woods, about how they had shown her the tunnel that led under the wall of the rectory and how Ali had been the one who had set off after her.

They had waited as long as they dared, hoping that Ali or Rose would reappear, but as the last remnants of day started to fade and the dark of the woods started to close around them, the children had finally lost their nerve and run.

Mervyn had flown off the handle at Billy. He was the eldest. How dare he just run off and leave a ten-year-old girl out there on her own? Beth had thought he was going to hit Billy, and that's when Jeff had waded into the argument to protect his son, and it had taken Bob Perry and several others in the pub to separate the two men.

Mervyn had shaken himself free and pulled on his jacket, prepared to head out into the night and confront Nathaniel Morton then and there. He had barely made it 100 metres across the dark car park at the back of the pub before the first of the night's creatures had driven him back.

That had been two hours ago and Mervyn had stood in the window, staring into the night, ever since. Beth had never seen him angrier or more despairing. She had tried to talk to him but the anguish on his face had frightened her more than she dared show. Now she tried to convince herself that Ali was a sensible girl. That she knew the dangers of the night and would find herself somewhere safe to hide until it was dawn.

Beth looked over at the clock that hung above the bar, watching the second hand making its way inexorably around the face. Dawn was such a long, long way away.

The door of the pub crashed open and Beth swung round in fearful anticipation. The Doctor breezed through with Bronwyn in his wake. He crossed to the bar, flashing a brilliant smile at Beth.

'I know!'

The assembled villagers watched him in open-mouthed amazement.

'I know how to deal with this. At least I know how to *start* to deal with this. Bronwyn's idea. Brilliant. But I need your help.'

Mervyn charged across the pub, catching the Doctor by the lapels of his coat and slamming him back against the wall.

'No, Mervyn!' screamed Beth. 'Don't.'

Jeff Palmer stepped forward. 'Don't be foolish, Mervyn.'

'The only foolish thing we've done has been to let this man and his friend anywhere near our daughter.' Mervyn Hardy's voice was shaking with rage.

The Doctor shook himself free from the big man's grip, looking round at the hostile faces in the pub.

'I haven't got time for this. Rose is in trouble and I need your help to rescue her.'

'Oh, so now you need our help,' Mervyn sneered contemptuously. 'You sent your friend up to the Morton place, and now she's trapped there, and our daughter with her!'

'You mean to say that Ali…' The Doctor looked from Mervyn to Beth in alarm.

Beth came out from behind the bar, her face pleading. 'You said you were going to help us. And now Ali is out there, like Mervyn said. With those things…'

Unable to hold it in any more, the tears started to

flood from her eyes. She buried her face in her husband's chest.

'Now listen to me.' The Doctor's voice rang strongly across the pub, confident and controlling. 'I said I would help and I meant it.'

'Help? Poking around on Black Island with that mad old bat.' Mervyn nodded at Bronwyn.

'Yes, poking around on Black Island. Very interesting poking. Interesting and informative poking that might just hold the key to what is going on here. We found machinery in the lighthouse –'

'That lighthouse hasn't been used for years,' Mervyn interrupted.

'Well, it's being used now! Perhaps if you'd done some poking of your own, you might have found that out for yourselves!'

'What sort of machinery?' asked Bob Perry.

'Alien machinery.' The Doctor kept his voice level. 'Alien machinery that affects the minds of your children, that keeps you docile and afraid and stops you thinking straight. Alien machinery that has paralysed you into inactivity.'

A low muttering went around the pub.

'Alien?' Bob snorted. 'What? You think you and your girlfriend are like those two from *The X-Files* or something?'

'Yes.'

'You're having a laugh.'

'Do I look like I'm laughing?'

'Now look, it's our daughter out there.' Mervyn's voice was low and dangerous. 'And she's –'

'Completely safe if we wake everyone up!' shouted the Doctor.

The pub went silent.

'The creatures are created by the children. That's one reason why you didn't want to call anyone for help, isn't it, Mrs Hardy? You worked it out. You knew that the creatures only appeared when your children fell asleep, and you were afraid. Afraid that if anyone found out your children would be taken away.'

The Doctor looked at the expectant faces surrounding him. 'Whatever is going on at the rectory relies on the dreams of the children. Not any adult dreams, not the dreams of babies, but the dreams of children. Young, imaginative children.'

The Doctor beamed at Billy Palmer. 'But what happens if we stop them going to sleep? No nightmares, no monsters.'

Mervyn snorted. 'Don't be daft, man. We can't stop them sleeping indefinitely!'

'Not indefinitely.' The Doctor rounded on him, looking him full in the face. 'Tonight. Just keep them awake for tonight and I will finish this once and for all. Keep them awake long enough to clear the woods of monsters, long enough for me to get to the rectory. Then I will rescue my friend and your daughter.'

Beth Hardy clutched at her husband's arm. 'Mervyn…'

Mervyn looked down at the frightened face of his wife for a long while, then nodded. 'Promise me this will work, Doctor.'

'It will,' said the Doctor. 'I promise.'

'What do you want us to do?'

The Doctor turned to the crowded pub. 'Go home, all of you. Go home and wake your kids up. Tell your neighbours to do the same. Get hold of anyone who has children and let them know. Get the kids out of bed. Let them watch television, drag out all their toys, play tiddlywinks with them, make them dance, make them sing.'

The Doctor bounded over to the jukebox, hauling a handful of coins from his pocket and pushing them into the machine. He punched at various buttons and 'Staying Alive' by the Bee Gees started to blare from the speakers.

'Play them records, give them chocolate, fizzy drinks, enough Tartrazene to have 'em bouncing off the walls! Anything! Just don't let them sleep. Starve Morton of what it is he needs!'

The Doctor crouched down next to Billy Palmer. 'This tunnel of yours, how do I get there?'

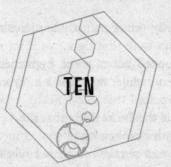

TEN

Rose eased the door open and peeked out into the corridor, checking to see if the coast was clear. Motioning to Ali to stay put, she stepped on to the landing, padding cautiously over to the banisters. The old house was dark and quiet, the only sound the muffled beep of the medical equipment from the dining room.

Rose peered down into the hallway, clutching at the banister rail for support. Her head was still spinning, the drugs that Peyne had pumped into her making her dizzy and nauseous. All she wanted to do was lie down and go to sleep, but she had to take the chance that Ali had given them. They weren't going to get a second go at this.

She had splashed handfuls of water on to her face from the little sink, desperately trying to shake the lethargy from her limbs. She had hoped that they might be able to escape through a window, shinning down a drainpipe or something into the garden, but the windows were shut tight, glued into their frames with year upon year of paint. Even if they had been able to open a window, it was a long way down and Rose wasn't sure that she'd make it in her current condition. It was more likely that she'd end up flat on her back with a broken leg or something.

No, they had to take the chance of getting out the same way they'd come in: down to the cellar and back out through the tunnel. Then she had to find the Doctor and let him know what she had found out. Which wasn't much. Other than discovering the truth about the masked nurses, she was no closer to finding out what Morton was actually up to.

She suddenly felt a surge of anger. Where the hell was the Doctor? Surely he had finished looking over the lighthouse by now? Surely he had noticed that she'd been gone hours?

'Rose?'

Ali was peeking through the crack in the door. As Rose turned to tell her to shut up, her foot caught on something and she nearly fell. She looked down to see what she had tripped over. Cables snaked up the side of the staircase, cutting across the polished wooden floor of the landing and vanishing down the corridor. Rose knelt down, puzzled. The cables wound across the hallway and vanished with a tangle of others through the wall into the dining room. She frowned.

Most of that wiring made its way down to the cellar, so where did this one go?

As Rose started to follow the winding cables, there was a squeak from Ali.

'Where are you going?'

Rose hurried back to her. 'I've found something. I just want to check it out.'

'You're not gonna leave me here, though!'

'I'll be two minutes.'

Ali caught her arm. 'Please!'

Rose sighed. Ali was right. She couldn't just leave her here. 'You still got that key?'

Ali pulled the heavy brass key from her pocket and held it out to Rose.

'Right. Let's try and delay them finding out we've gone for a while.'

Rose locked the door, then slipped the key into her back pocket. Hopefully when the nurses next came to collect her they would forget that they'd left the key in the lock and spend precious moments searching for it. That might give her and Ali some extra time to work out where the cables went and get out of the house.

'Right,' said Rose. 'Now, follow me, but quiet.'

The two of them crept along the corridor, wincing at every creak of the ancient floorboards. If anything the upper part of the house had seen less maintenance than the lower level. Wallpaper bulged alarmingly in several areas and huge brown patches on the once white ceiling showed that water was getting in from somewhere.

The floor was thick with dust and footprints were clearly visible down the length of the corridor, following the trail of cable and wiring. Rose strained to hear any sign of life, but her head was still muzzy, her ears ringing.

They rounded a corner. The corridor in front of them ended at a tall, elegant door, its once pristine varnish now scuffed and faded. A ragged hole had been torn through the wall next to the frame and the cables wound their way through the broken plaster.

Rose chewed her lip nervously. The corridor was a dead end. If someone came up behind them now, they would be trapped, but she was damned if she was going to leave without finding out what was on the other side of that door.

A sudden thought struck her. When she had been at the back of the house she'd noticed a fire escape. If she had the layout of the house right... She crossed to a window and peered out into the wet night. The fire escape was right there! Rose gave a smile of satisfaction. They wouldn't have to go out through the cellar after all. If only the window would open.

She pulled at the catch. It was stiff but it moved.

Ali gave her a curious look.

'What are you doing?'

'Getting us a way out, I hope,' said Rose. 'Let's see if

our luck is holding, shall we?'

She gripped the bottom of the old sash window and heaved. With a terrible rattle, it slid upwards. Cold air and rain swirled in.

Rose could have cried with relief. She stuck her head out of the window. The courtyard below was dark and empty. A badly fixed security light banged back and forth in the wind, sending fingers of light dancing across the wet flagstones.

Rose ducked back inside, crouching down and gripping Ali by the shoulders.

'Right. There's a ladder out there. A fire escape. I want you to climb down, get over to the tunnel and go!'

Ali looked frightened. 'What about you? What are you going to do?'

'I need to look inside that room.' Rose nodded over at the door. 'As soon as I've seen what's inside, then I'll follow you.'

Ali shook her head. 'I want to stay with you.'

'No.' Rose's voice was stern. 'You've got to go! If I don't get out, if they get me again, then you have to find the Doctor and tell him where I am.' She ruffled Ali's hair. 'I need you to do this for me. I need to know that you're safe. OK?'

Ali thought for a moment, then nodded solemnly.

'Good girl.'

Rose caught Ali under the arms and swung her up

on to the window sill. Ali grimaced as rain splashed against her face, ducked through the window and carefully lowered herself down on to the metal platform of the fire escape. The ladder vibrated alarmingly.

'It doesn't feel very safe.' Ali looked up at Rose nervously.

'You'll be fine.' Rose tried to sound confident. 'These things always wobble a bit. Now go. Quick as you can!'

She watched as Ali turned and made her way unsteadily down the rickety fire escape, brushing her wet hair out of her eyes. She reached the bottom and hovered nervously next to the wall of the house, staring at the dark courtyard. Then, with a last look up at Rose, she dashed across to the lean-to, splashing through the water that was pooled on the flagstones.

The little girl reached the shed and, with a little wave back up at the house, vanished from view. Rose gave a sigh of relief. She was safe. From the aliens inside the house at any rate. The dark woods were ominous and oppressive, but for the moment they were mercifully free of the roars and shrieks of the creatures. Ali was a smart girl and she knew the woods like the back of her hand. She'd get home OK... wouldn't she?

Desperately trying to convince herself that she was doing the right thing, Rose pulled her head back inside and slid the window closed. The cold rain and fresh air had cleared her head a little and the sickness in her stomach was slowly fading. Brushing her hair back, she crept down the corridor to the door, pressing her ear up against it and listening for sounds of movement from within.

She frowned. She couldn't hear movement, but rather something that sounded like... breathing.

She pulled back from the door, unsure about what to do. Perhaps the six ancient figures downstairs weren't the only patients that Morton had locked away.

Tentatively she reached out for the brass door handle. It turned easily and the door swung open. Rose stepped into the room beyond.

And felt the scream start to build in her throat.

The big Range Rover swung into the estate, lights blazing, and pulled up on the edge of the wood in a shower of spray. The passenger door swung open and the Doctor bounded out into the rain.

'OK, you wait here and keep an eye out for us. If anything with big pointy teeth comes out of the woods, leg it!'

Mervyn nodded, his face grim. The Doctor gave him a reassuring smile. The drive up from the pub had been a fraught one. The children were waking up, but it was taking a while and a few monsters still stalked the streets. The dent in the side door and the thick, dark ichor that was splashed across the bonnet of the Range Rover evidence of a closer encounter with one of the creatures than either Mervyn or the Doctor had wanted.

'Doctor, I'm sorry.' Mervyn held out an apologetic hand. 'For earlier…'

'Oh, don't worry.' The Doctor shook his hand vigorously. 'I do this sort of thing all the time!' Then, with a broad grin, he slammed the door and vanished into the trees.

Mervyn watched him go. 'Yes, I'm beginning to believe that,' he muttered finally.

Peyne tapped at the controls in front of her in puzzlement. Readings were slowly shutting down across the board. One by one, read-outs were starting to drop to tick-over levels, lights going dark on banks of instruments.

She glanced over at the others. Her technicians were darting from console to console, the once quiet air of efficiency starting to acquire a tinge of panic.

'Hadron!' she barked at one of the hurrying figures. 'What is happening?'

The masked figure quickly came over. 'We're not sure, Priest Commander.' The voice was muffled and indistinct.

Peyne tore off Hadron's mask with an angry snarl.

'What do you mean you're not sure? Subconscious brainwave activity energy is dropping to unsustainable levels!'

'Yes, Priest Commander.' The Cynrog technician shuffled under her glare, forked tongue flicking across his thin lips. 'But the fault is not here. The fault seems to lie with the imagers themselves.'

'Impossible!' snarled Peyne, thrusting the flaccid human mask back at him. 'Check the generators! At once!'

As Hadron saluted sharply and hurried out of the ward, Peyne turned angrily back to the dropping readouts. The Synod was relying on her. The entire campaign plans of the Cynrog rested with her. All had been going exactly as planned until now. Until the arrival of this interfering Time Lord. She gritted her teeth. They could not fail now. Not when they were so close to completion, so close to being able to leave this primitive backwater planet. She longed to feel dry sand under her feet again and the warmth of the suns on her skin, not this constant grinding dampness.

She wriggled uncomfortably in her human disguise. She wanted to be free of the constraints of this unpleasant body and the constant irritation of Nathaniel Morton. But she would do her duty; she would complete her mission.

Abandoning her useless controls in frustration, she crossed the ward to one of the sleeping figures. Her nose wrinkled in disgust. These humans were weak, feeble things, susceptible to every disease the planet had to offer. It amazed her that they survived at all, let alone that they made it into old age like these pathetic specimens. But for now the humans were necessary. More than that, they were essential and so she would bide her time. When the moment came she would enjoy the subjugation of this miserable planet. She would enjoy watching Balor destroy it if he saw fit.

She ran a hand over the forehead of the sleeping figure.

'Soon, Balor,' she hissed. 'Soon.'

Rose stared in fascinated horror at the room. It was huge and very dark, a library by the look of things: bookcases on every wall, the shelves piled high with ancient, dusty tomes. Like practically every other room in the house, the furniture had been cleared away and the resulting empty space adapted to another purpose.

Here the once elegant antique tables now groaned under the weight of alien machinery, lights glimmering in the gloom. The thick cables that wound into the room coiled their way up the tall bookcases, splitting and dividing, spreading out through the room like a tangled spider's web, looping their way to four heavy, ugly clusters of alien technology, one hanging in each corner of the room.

Energy crackled from the machines, sending flickering fingers of electricity arcing across the library. There was a smell like summer lightning. And hanging in the midst of the lightning was the *thing*.

Rose took a tentative step into the room, trying to get a better view through the dancing spears of light. The thing was huge, a mass of glistening flesh hanging suspended in the electrical web. Rose rubbed at her eyes. It was difficult to make out its shape properly. One minute she thought she could see scales and ridged skin, the next it looked like fur or, worse, like dead, pale human flesh.

Goosebumps ran across her skin and she felt the hairs at the back of her neck stand on end. Her heart was pounding in her chest, her breathing becoming faster and faster. She forced herself closer to the monstrous shape. Every fibre of her being screamed at her to run, to get out of this place as fast as her legs would carry her, to run and not look back, to hide from this monstrosity before it reached out for her and dragged her into that horrible crackling web.

She swallowed hard, trying to control the fear that threatened to overwhelm her. She had to let the Doctor know what was going on. He was relying on her and she wasn't going to let him down.

She forced herself to take a step closer, then another. Waves of energy seemed to ripple across the creature, almost changing its shape as they washed around it. Horns and claws and tusks seemed to appear and disappear across the writhing skin. One minute it looked almost humanoid, the next it was something hunched and animal-like. High above her, almost pressed against the ceiling, Rose thought she could make out the shape of a head of some kind. Shadows flitted this way and that, making it difficult to see. She leaned closer. She had to get a proper look.

The creature's eyes flicked open.

The Doctor raced through the wood, branches whipping at him as he followed the line of the old rectory wall. The villagers were now integral to his plan, giving him time. With the kids awake, the woods would be safe, and no monsters to avoid meant that he didn't need to be stealthy. But it also meant that whatever was going on at the rectory would now be interrupted, and that probably wouldn't be a good thing for Rose. He had to get inside quickly, preferably unseen. Ali's mysterious tunnel seemed like the best way.

If all went the way that he hoped, then Morton's plans would be interrupted until morning. It was unfortunate that he had so many disparate elements to deal with. The lighthouse was out of the way and tricky to get to – which was no doubt why they had used it to house the transmitters in the first place – the rectory was tucked away on the cliff tops and Bronwyn was down in the village.

The Doctor still wasn't certain how Bronwyn Ceredig fitted into the puzzle, but she was part of it, of that he had no doubt. Bronwyn, Nathaniel Morton and a small boy called Jimmy who was almost certainly Bronwyn's son. All of them pieces of a puzzle he still had to solve...

'In between rescuing Rose and Ali, dismantling the transmitters and stopping all this ever happening again. I *do* love holidays by the sea!'

The tangle of rhododendron bushes and broken brickwork that Billy Palmer had told him about loomed out of the darkness. The Doctor pushed his way through the wet leaves and into the remains of the old coalbunker. The tunnel entrance was only partially concealed. Billy had said that they'd left in a hurry.

The Doctor pulled the sodden plywood to one side, peering into the dark.

'Cold, wet tunnel... just my sort of thing!'

His sonic screwdriver flared into life, casting a bright blue glow into the gloom, and the Doctor dived inside.

Rose ran faster than she could ever have believed possible. She made no attempt at concealment; she just wanted to put as much distance as possible between herself and the nightmare in the library.

When the thing had opened its eyes Rose had felt such fear and dread and total despair that she thought her legs were going to give way beneath her. As the cold, black gaze had swept over her, every nightmare and every bad moment of her life had bubbled up from the places in her memory where they had been hidden. She had started to shake uncontrollably, too frightened to cry or to scream. All warmth had left her, all hope; she was cold and empty and alone, abandoned, at the mercy of this thing.

She had screwed her eyes up, waiting for the final blow, for teeth and claws to tear into her flesh, but that blow never came. She forced herself to open her eyes again, physically flinching under the silent gaze of the towering monster.

The eyes were dead. Vacant. Nothing had glimmered in those cold black orbs: no intelligence, no life, nothing. The creature was a shell, a vessel. It couldn't see her, but somehow that made it even more frightening.

And so Rose had run. She had turned and fled from that room, tearing down the long corridor, throwing open the window and escaping into the night. She had almost broken her neck on the fire escape. The metal was wet and slippery and her feet had slid away from her a couple of times, sending her tumbling down the steep stairs. She had hit the courtyard running and hadn't looked back, diving headfirst into the tunnel.

Only now, in the cool dark, did she finally start to slow down, aware that if she carried on in her manic flight she was liable to fall headfirst into the mud and brain herself on the wet brickwork.

She dropped to her knees, oblivious to the freezing

water, her breath coming in great ragged gulps. She hated herself for running, hated herself for being unable to stand her ground. After all she'd been through! But most of the things she had faced somehow paled into insignificance beside the terror she had felt in the library.

'What are you up to Morton? What the *hell* are you up to?'

Ali sat in the dark tunnel, banging her torch against the palm of her hand in frustration. The blinking light from the LEDs had been fine when she'd reached the safety of the tunnel, but as she'd progressed further and further into the inky depths it had started to falter. Now she could only get any light if she turned the torch off and then back on again, and even then it only lasted for a few seconds.

Hunkering down against the tunnel wall, she unscrewed the back of the little keyring and carefully pulled out the two tiny watch batteries. She clasped them in the palm of her hand, trying to warm them up. Whenever the TV remote control had failed at home, she had seen her father take the back of the handset and roll the batteries back and forth in their housing to get them working again. She desperately hoped that warming the torch batteries would give them enough power to get her to the end of the tunnel and safety.

She squinted, trying to make out any shapes around her, but the blackness was total. She had been walking for four or five minutes when the torch went out so she figured she was about halfway down the tunnel.

Even though she was more frightened than she had ever been in her life, Ali was hugely proud of herself. She knew that she'd have some explaining to do to her mum, and she didn't even want to think about how angry her dad was going to be, but the rest of the gang… They were going to be well impressed, and there was no way that Dai Barraclough was ever going to be able to tease her again, not after he'd run off like a startled rabbit.

In the dark Ali allowed herself a little smile. But that swiftly faded as the sound of something further down the tunnel reached her. Had one of the monsters entered the tunnel behind her? The noises were getting louder and louder. Whatever it was was coming fast.

Ali clambered to her feet. She could hear splashing footfalls echoing down the tunnel and the sound of laboured breathing. She started to back away, fumbling with the batteries. The tunnel was too small to hide in. In her panic the batteries slipped from her grasp. She heard them splash into the water that trickled through the drain. With a cry of despair she dropped to her knees, fingers raking through the slime. The noises behind her were getting closer and closer.

In terror, Ali abandoned the batteries and started to run. She could see nothing and her feet threatened to slide from under her at every step. She ran with her arms outstretched, desperately trying to balance herself against the wet walls. Her ankle caught on something and she went flying, bouncing off the tunnel wall and diving headlong into the freezing water. Sharp pain shot through her shin, but ignoring it she scrambled to her feet and continued her headlong flight. She didn't care what her parents or friends thought of her now; she just wanted to get out of this tunnel, out into the open air and away from whatever horror was in here with her.

Her eyes blurred with tears. As Ali made to brush them away with her sleeve, she cannoned into something tall and dark.

And screamed.

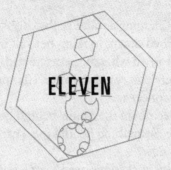

ELEVEN

Ali bit and screamed and flailed at the thing that had caught her, lashing out with her fists and feet. She could see nothing as the darkness was total, but the thing that had her was tall and gangly and she could hear it gasp in pain as her blows connected.

'Ow! Careful! You're going to do me some serious damage.'

It was a most un-monster-like voice.

Ali stopped struggling and an electric blue light lit up the tunnel. Rose's friend the Doctor stood there. He held a slim tube, like a torch, and the blue light was flaring from its tip.

'You're stronger than you look,' he said, hunching over, wincing in pain and rubbing at his knee.

Ali slapped his arm.

'Ow! What was that for?'

'You scared me!'

'Well, you scared me too!' The Doctor was indignant.

'Honestly. Charging about like that. Took years off me.'

He crouched down, looking her full in the face. Ali suddenly realised what nice eyes he had.

'What were you running from?' His voice was gentle and full of concern.

Ali pointed down the tunnel behind her. 'Something down there. Something behind me. I can hear it.'

'Can you now?'

The Doctor cocked his head to one side, listening. In the quiet dark the splashing footsteps were clear.

'Hear it?' whispered Ali. 'I think it's one of the monsters.'

'Do you? Well, it's your lucky day.' The Doctor stood up, pulling his coat straight. ''Cause I'm the Doctor, and if there's one thing that I do well, it's monsters.'

He held out the silver tube, pointing the glowing tip down the tunnel. Ali huddled behind him, staring into the shadows cast by the bright blue light. The splashing was getting louder and louder. She could just make out a shape in the dark. She screwed her eyes up, wondering what exactly the Doctor was going to do.

'Rose!'

The Doctor's voice was like a gunshot in the dark. He stood in the glare of the blue light from his sonic screwdriver.

Ali's face peered out from behind his legs. The little girl was drenched with filthy water, but the relief on her face mirrored that on Rose's own.

The Doctor splashed forward and gave her an enormous hug.

'Hello, you! I was just coming to get you!'

She hugged him back gratefully.

'Talk about leaving it until just *after* the nick of time.'

'Sorry. Got a bit caught up.'

Ali hurried over to them and Rose tousled her hair. 'I thought I told you to get out of here.'

'My torch packed up.'

'She thought you were a monster.' The Doctor grinned. 'Personally, I think that's a bit harsh...'

'Hey!' Rose frowned at him.

The Doctor winked at Ali, then caught Rose by the arm, leading her a little way down the tunnel.

'I've been worried about you. We had some... interesting visitors out on Black Island. Some old friends conjured out of the ether. Slitheen, Daleks, that sort of thing...' All flippancy had gone from his voice now. 'Do I gather that Mr Nathaniel Morton has been a less than perfect host?'

Rose nodded, and proceeded to tell him everything that had happened since she had made it into the cellar, grateful for the chance to finally unburden herself to someone who might understand what was going on.

The Doctor listened, his face hard and his jaw tightening as Rose described the mind-scan that Morton and the others had subjected her to. When she finally reached the thing in the library, she lowered her voice so as not to alarm Ali. The little girl had already been through enough; she didn't need to know that the worst monster was still to come.

The Doctor stroked his chin thoughtfully. 'Cynrog. That's not good.'

'You've met them?'

'Not met them, but know them by reputation. Not a very nice reputation either.'

'And they've got a thing about frightening children, have they?'

'No, that's the bit that's puzzling. The equipment is nothing that the Cynrog aren't capable of. But they're behaving oddly. All this sneaking about, hiding under masks… not like them at all.'

'So how should they be?'

'Oh, I dunno. Stamping about and giving orders. Blowing things up. That sort of thing… They're warriors, subjugating the galaxy in the name of their great all-powerful god.' He frowned, looking almost disappointed.

'Well, let's just count ourselves lucky that they're not stamping around, blowing things up, shall we?' Rose said. 'What are we gonna do about stopping them?'

'First things first.' The Doctor pulled a crumpled photograph from his pocket. 'Look familiar?'

Rose took it, squinting at it in the dim light. It was the photograph of a small boy.

'Oh, my God! It's the boy I saw in my dream.'

'I've been seeing a lot of him tonight. It seems that it's not just monsters being brought to life.'

'Where did you get this?'

'Bronwyn Ceredig. Now, I need you to find out who this is… I think his name is Jimmy and I think he was her son. Find out what happened to him, Rose. Find out what Bronwyn knows.'

'You think she's something to do with this?'

'That's what I need you to find out! What I *do* know is that there's a thumping great alien transmitter in the lamp room of the lighthouse that needs sorting out.' The Doctor smiled that mischievous smile of his. 'And that's where young Ali here comes in.'

Peyne stared in frustration at the inert equipment that littered the cellar. All around it, Cynrog technicians scurried to and fro, pushing past her without catching her gaze. Psychic reception had fallen practically to zero.

Hadron hurried over to her.

'Well?' Peyne snapped.

'The equipment is functioning perfectly, Priest Commander. And the generators are at full power. If we are not receiving a signal, then it can only mean that…'

'That the children are not asleep.' Peyne gave a hiss of displeasure.

'You think they have realised?'

'The primitives in the village have no concept of what is going on. No, I think our friend the Doctor has had a hand in this. A Time Lord desperately trying to uphold the principles of his people. Protecting the lesser species.' Peyne's voice was filled with contempt.

'Do we still have his companion, the girl?'

'Yes, Commander Peyne. Locked in one of the upper rooms.'

'Then the Doctor might regret siding with these humans.' She licked her lips with a flick of her tongue. 'Can the equipment be modified to *induce* sleep in the target subjects?'

Hadron's brow furrowed. 'Theoretically it is just a matter of recalibration of some of the components in the emitter.'

'Then do it! Force the children back into their dream state. The Synod will not wait much longer and I am keen to be free of this world.'

'Peyne?' Morton's voice bellowed from upstairs.

Peyne hissed in irritation.

'Peyne, I want to talk to you!'

'I expect a report from you in fifteen minutes, Priest Technician Hadron.' Peyne's voice made it perfectly clear that she would brook no more delays. 'Take as many novices as you need from other duties to get the work done, but get those children dreaming again!'

Hadron hurried back towards the machinery, summoning technicians as he went. Peyne turned and made her way up the cellar stairs.

Morton was waiting for her at the top.

'What is going on, Peyne?'

The old man's face was red and beaded with sweat. Peyne wrinkled her nose in disgust.

She shut the door to the cellar, determined to keep her tone civil. She still needed Morton's cooperation, at least for the present. It would do them no good for the man to get unduly agitated.

'It seems our friend the Doctor has some understanding of what we are doing here, of how we are generating the creatures at any rate. It seems that he has persuaded our dreamers not to sleep tonight.'

Morton's hands tightened on the arms of his wheelchair, knuckles whitening.

'Why is he interfering?'

Peyne gave an unpleasant smile. 'Because he's a Time Lord. He thinks that it is his role to put right the wrongs of the universe. They always were an arrogant race and this one is no different.'

'Damn him!'

There was anguish in Morton's voice. It was this anguish that was responsible for what they had started here, this anguish that Peyne had used to drive Morton ever further, that had brought them here to this ancient rectory and so close to completing her mission.

It had made Morton ambitious and dangerous.

'Is the Doctor's friend still locked up?' he snapped.

Peyne nodded. 'In one of the upper rooms.'

'Then get her! Bring her down here.' Morton was shaking with rage. 'If the Doctor insists on interfering, then he and the girl will regret it.'

Peyne gave a smile of amusement. It never ceased to amaze her how far this primitive was prepared to go for his own survival. She had chosen wisely when she picked him.

'The technicians are busy. I'll get the girl myself.'

'Bring her to the ward.'

With that Morton spun his wheelchair on the spot and wheeled himself out of the hallway. She liked seeing him like this. Too often he moped and moaned his way through the day, constantly whining about his condition. Anger made him powerful, anger let her see what lay within him, and it thrilled her.

She crossed the hall, climbing the old staircase to the upper floor. It might be interesting to let Morton have free rein with the girl, to see just how far he was prepared to go. If nothing else, it would provide the technicians with a much needed diversion from the monotony of their duties.

She crossed to the door of the room where the girl was locked and pulled the snub-nosed disintegrator pistol from her pocket. The girl should still be groggy from the drugs that she had been given, but there was no harm in being cautious. She reached out to open the door then stopped, puzzled. The key wasn't in the lock. She reached for the brass handle and turned it. There was a soft click. The door was unlocked!

With a cry of anger, Peyne kicked the door open and stopped in amazement.

Sprawled out on the bed, arms folded behind his head, was the Doctor.

He sat up unhurriedly and gave her a quizzical look. 'Room service, I hope. I'd love a cuppa.'

Snarling, Peyne raised the gun.

Beth Hardy looked up from her work as she heard the heavy rumble of her husband's Range Rover in the car park. She placed the glass she had been washing back on the bar and wiped her wet hands on her apron.

She had taken down every single glass from the shelf above the bar and washed them, one by one, then polished them until they gleamed and put them back again. The job had taken hours. It was stupid, but it was the only thing she could think of to take her mind off Ali.

After the Doctor's speech, the bar had emptied quickly, everyone hurrying back to their homes to wake their children and their neighbour's children. Outside, the village was now a cacophony of music and air horns. Someone had even found a box of fireworks from somewhere – Eric Molson from the corner shop probably – and the occasional bang from some of the bigger rockets was still rattling the windows in their frames. In among the noise was something that had not been heard for a long time in Ynys Du: the sound of children laughing.

A few had returned to the pub, their children in tow. Tables all across the bar were scattered with board games hauled from Ali's bedroom, and the restaurant had been turned into an impromptu dance floor. Parents and children alike jiggled and danced to a collection of 1950s classics. Somewhat appropriately, 'Rock Around the Clock' was playing at the moment.

Beth watched as a young boy, the youngest of Bob Perry's kids, slumped into a chair in the corner of the lounge bar, rubbing at his eyes with the sleeve of his dressing gown and giving a huge yawn. Almost immediately his mother was at his side, hauling him back to his feet and twirling him out on to the dance floor. Beth could see the determination in her false smile, hear the strain in her laughter. Most of the children were young and already tired by week after week of troubled sleep. They simply weren't going to be able to keep them all awake for ever. Sooner or later one of them was going to give in to their fatigue, and then the things would start to appear again.

Beth closed her eyes and whispered a silent prayer. She had realised almost immediately the connection between the monsters and the children. She had seen things that Ali had drawn in her sketchpad and written about in her notebook stalking down the high street, all claws and teeth and childish colour schemes. These things hadn't been real creatures; they were children's monsters, combinations of every dark fairytale, every schoolyard horror story, every half-glimpsed late-night movie.

What had scared her more than the monsters was the thought of some government agency arriving to investigate, some faceless bureaucrat bundling Ali into the back of a van and taking her away. Beth had also been having nightmares since all this had started, but hers were not of monsters. In hers her daughter lay in a sterile hospital room, tubes and needles littered across her skin, faceless men in white coats prodding and pulling at her. She wasn't going to let that happen.

And so she had kept her fears to herself, not talking to her friends, not talking to her husband. She was sure that most if not all of her neighbours suspected the same as her. Half-finished conversations, furtive nods, smiles of sympathy, but no one with the courage to do anything. They had made the monsters part of their normal lives, fitting them into their nightly routine, as familiar as brushing teeth or putting the cat out.

Beth almost laughed out loud. It was ludicrous. The entire village had tried to convince itself that nothing was wrong, but the truth was that everything was horribly, terribly wrong, only they were powerless to stop it. If the Doctor was right, then they were being manipulated, controlled by the machinery in the lighthouse, chained to the village, kept afraid and impotent, too scared to help themselves.

But now the Doctor was here, now they weren't alone.

He had been heading out of the front door when Mervyn had shrugged on his jacket and offered to drive him up to the rectory. The Doctor had given him a dazzling smile and in that moment Beth had known that everything *would* be all right, that he really was going to bring their daughter back.

That had seemed like hours ago, and ever since she had been cleaning glasses, straining to hear past the music and the din outside, waiting for the sound of their car pulling into its parking spot.

She crossed to the back door and pulled back the net curtains. The headlights from the car were dazzling her. She couldn't see properly...

Then the headlights snapped off, the passenger door sprang open and a small figure emerged.

Beth cried out, hauled the door open and rushed into the rain. Ali stood caked in mud with a guilty look on her face, the look she always had if she'd just been caught raiding the sweet jar or reading by torchlight under the covers of her bed.

Beth swept her up into her arms, oblivious to the mud, not sure whether to laugh or cry. Ali squirmed in her grip, embarrassed.

'I'm all right, Mum.'

'Quite a handful, your Ali.'

Beth looked up. The Doctor's friend, Rose, was standing there shivering. Her face was pale and streaked with dirt. She looked exhausted.

'Thank you.' Beth could feel her vision blurring. 'Thank you so much for bringing her back.'

Rose shuffled uncomfortably. 'Yeah, well, don't thank me too soon. This isn't over yet, and I don't think you're gonna like the next bit.'

'No.'

Beth curled a protective arm around her daughter's shoulder, her face a mixture of anger and disbelief.

'You can't ask us to do that. Not again.'

Rose sighed. She had known that this was going to be the tricky bit ever since the Doctor had outlined his plan. They were sitting in the old-fashioned kitchen of the pub, a welcome refuge from the cacophony of the bar. Ali sat draped in an old tartan blanket, a huge mug of hot chocolate in her hands. Her parents sat protectively on either side of her. They had barely let her out of their sight since she had got back inside the house.

Rose had changed into an old sweatshirt and some tracksuit bottoms that Beth had lent her, feeling warm for the first time in what seemed like an age. She drained the last dregs of coffee from her mug.

'Look, I know that this is hard for you, but the Doctor says…'

'The Doctor says…' Mervyn slammed his palm down on the table, sending cutlery flying. 'He went up there to rescue Ali and now you just want to put her in danger again?'

'She's not going to be in any danger!' Rose was getting exasperated now. 'I told you, there's a transmitter in the old lighthouse. That's what's been causing the nightmares. That's what's been controlling you, stopping you sorting this out for yourselves. All we've got to do is knock it out and the Cynrog are powerless.'

'The Cynrog.' Mervyn snorted. 'Aliens with masks that live in the rectory.'

'Yes! Disable the transmitter and it stops whatever they're up to.'

'Then why don't I just go up there with a big hammer and smash the thing?'

'No!' Rose banged her mug down. 'That won't help.'

The Doctor had explained to her that simply destroying the transmitter wasn't going to do any good. Worse, it might trigger something that affected the kids permanently. It had to be disabled carefully and precisely, he had been very clear about that. She reached into her pocket and pulled out the sonic screwdriver, placing it on the dining table in front of her.

'This is what's gonna do the job. This and someone

small enough to get where it needs to be used.' She nodded at Ali. 'She can do it. Just let her come with me and we can finish this.'

'No.'

'Mr Hardy…'

'I said no!' Mervyn rose to his feet, knocking his chair backwards. 'I'm warning you, girl…'

'Or what?' Rose could feel her own anger building now. 'What are you gonna do? Hit me? Throw me out? We're the ones trying to help you. Me and the Doctor. If you're too stupid to listen to what we have to say…'

'Stop it!' Ali's voice was shrill and piercing. 'Stop it, stop it, stop it!'

She pulled at her father's sleeve. 'Why are you shouting at Rose, Dad? She can stop it. She and the Doctor can stop the monsters!'

Mervyn stared down at his daughter, not knowing what to say to her. Ali leaned across and picked up the sonic screwdriver, turning it over in her hand carefully. She looked up at Rose.

'Can this thing really fix everything? Make it like it was before?'

Rose nodded. 'The Doctor's told me exactly what he wants us to do, but we've got to hurry.'

Ali hopped down off her chair. 'Well, let's go, then.'

'Ali, no…'

Mervyn reached out for his daughter, but she stepped away from him.

'Dad, I don't want nightmares every night. I'm tired of being afraid to go to sleep and letting the monsters get out. I want to be able to play with my friends without being scared. I don't want you and Mum worrying about me.'

She looked over to her mother. 'Mum, I know you cry every night. I don't want you to be unhappy because of me. Rose and the Doctor can put it right. I want to do something to help. Please. Let me do something. I'm not a little girl any more.'

She turned to Rose. 'What is it that you want me to do?'

The Doctor watched as Morton hauled himself painfully up the stairs, step after agonising step, towards the wheelchair that waited for him on the landing. One of the masked Cynrog reached down to help him, but he batted the proffered hand away angrily and slumped breathless into the ancient metal-framed chair.

The Doctor studied the old man carefully. He had refused all offers of help, determined to make the climb on his own. Peyne had rung down to his office from the cumbersome old phone that sat on the table on the landing. The Doctor hadn't heard what had been said on the other end, but it wasn't difficult to work out.

Then Peyne had stood in the doorway of the room,

her unpleasant little disintegrator gun pointed squarely at the Doctor's chest, patiently waiting as Morton made his creaking progress up the once grand staircase.

'Stubborn, isn't he?' the Doctor whispered conspiratorially to Peyne as Morton wiped his brow. He raised his voice. 'You should get a stair lift. Make things much easier in a big place like this. Get Miss Peyne here to send for a catalogue.'

Morton wheeled himself over to where the Doctor stood, staring up at him with contempt. 'Always keen on airing your ideas, aren't you, Doctor?'

'Oh, you'll find I'm full of good ideas, Mr Morton. Bursting with 'em. Every one a winner.'

'But you're not a winner, Doctor, and it is we who are bursting with ideas. At this very moment Miss Peyne and her colleagues are working hard to put right the little hiccup that you've created and then, I'm afraid, it's business as usual.'

'And what might your business be, Mr Morton?' The Doctor dropped down on to his haunches, bringing his face level with Morton's. 'Allying yourself with the Cynrog? Filling the lighthouse with psychic transmitters? Oh yes, I've been doing a little digging, turning up all sorts of interesting things, and I really don't like what I'm finding. Not one little bit.'

He leaned closer to Morton, staring him full in the face.

'But what's it all for, eh? You're not doing all this just to terrify a village full of children.'

'It is a... necessary evil, Doctor.'

'No, Nathaniel, it is not necessary.' The Doctor's voice was low and dangerous now, all sense of flippancy gone. 'It is very unnecessary. It is a sick, twisted game and it is going to stop.'

'You think so, Doctor? You think you have all the answers?' A grim smile flickered over Morton's lined face. 'Well, come and see the prize in our... game, as you put it.'

Morton spun his wheelchair and rolled across the landing. Peyne pushed the barrel of her blaster into the back of the Doctor's neck, catching him by the collar and hauling him to his feet. She marched him along the corridor, following Morton and his creaking chair.

'I'm told that your people were well travelled, Doctor.' The old man's voice echoed down the dusty corridor. 'That they roamed the reaches of time and space, eternally youthful. My own short span has had precious little youth, and the breadth of my wandering has been confined to this one small planet, but look at what we have created.'

He threw open the doors of the library.

'Behold, the great Balor! Dark God of the Cynrog, Destroyer of Worlds!'

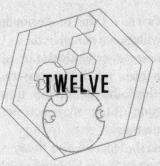

TWELVE

The Doctor stepped into the crackling, electrically charged air of the library and gave a whistle of admiration.

'Oh, now that's impressive. Really, really impressive. I'm gonna give you eleven out of ten for that. Building a big monster in the library. A really *big* monster.'

He pulled out his glasses and perched them on the end of his nose, peering at the monstrosity that hung among the lightning flashes. 'Doesn't seem quite finished to me, though. Lacking a few final touches, hm?'

He paced slowly around the creature, squinting through the flickering light, watching as waves of energy rolled across it, modifying its form with every pass.

'Can't quite make your mind up on the details by the look of it. I mean, I know what it's like choosing a body you're happy with!'

He dived over to a cluster of silver machinery on one of the tables, hefting a bunch of cables in his hands.

'Lot of power being channelled up here.' He sniffed at the cable, then ran his tongue along it. 'Mmm, psychomorphic radiation! Psychomorphic! Honestly! Anyone would think that you were trying to manufacture a body.'

He dropped the cables with a bang.

'That's it, isn't it? You're building a body, but that's all it is at the moment – a body, a shell, a vessel.' He snapped his fingers at the creature. 'Oi! Big fella! Anyone home?'

The creature didn't stir. The Doctor turned back to Morton thoughtfully.

'A decidedly empty vessel.'

Morton clapped his hands slowly. 'Bravo, Doctor, bravo.'

'What's it for, Morton?'

'As you have correctly surmised, Doctor, it is – or rather, it nearly is – a body manufactured for inhabitation by a new soul.'

'But for whose soul?' The Doctor cast a wary look at Peyne. 'You mentioned the name Balor. I seem to remember a rather unpleasant figure from Cynrog mythology named Balor. Now, let me see if I've got this right. Balor, the general of the Cynrog hordes, left for dead after the battle of Grantran Prime, then revived through one of your questionable accelerated genetic-mutation experiments and revered as a god. Something like that anyway. I do hope you haven't been having RE lessons from Miss Peyne here?'

Peyne hissed unpleasantly. 'Be respectful in the way you refer to our god, Time Lord.'

'You *have* been listening to Miss Peyne. That's a great shame…'

'On the contrary, Doctor, Peyne has been a great comfort to me over the years.'

'Nathaniel, listen to me.' The Doctor's voice was urgent now. 'Whatever Peyne has told you, whatever she has promised you, the Cynrog are not to be trusted. They are vicious, brutal killers, they –'

'They saved my life, Doctor! My life and the lives of all those in the ward!'

'What?' The Doctor eyed Peyne suspiciously. 'What possible reason could you have for getting involved in human affairs? What are you doing with those people downstairs?'

'You understand nothing, Doctor.' There was contempt in the Cynrog commander's voice. 'You are so typical of your race, blundering in with your high moral stance, acting as judge and jury to the universe. We are well rid of your kind.'

'Doctor, listen to me!' Morton's voice was pleading now. 'Listen to the reasons for this. Perhaps then you will have some understanding of what we have had to endure. Of what *I* have had to endure.'

The Doctor fixed Morton with a piercing gaze. 'Tell me.'

Morton leaned back in his chair, his eyes misting with remembrance. 'I was ten years old. My cousin had come to Ynys Du with my aunt and uncle, a holiday by the sea.'

The Doctor did a quick calculation. 'The 1930s?'

'It was 1935. A glorious summer. We were full of the joys of youth, Doctor. Seven of us, good friends, happy children, not so different from those that play in the streets of Ynys Du today.'

'Except that you and your friends weren't tormented by creatures.'

'Oh, but we were, Doctor. Tormented by a creature more terrible than you can imagine.'

'What happened to you, Morton?' The Doctor's voice was gentler now. 'What did you see?'

'The seven of us had left our parents in the village. They were too busy with their gossip and their shopping. And my father and uncle were far too interested in the local beer to pay any attention to their errant offspring. We made our way up towards the cliff top – Ynys Du was a good deal smaller then, the woods closer, a haven of cool shadows. My cousin was never a good influence. He had stolen half a dozen cigarettes from my uncle's jacket pocket. It had been our intention to hide in the woods and smoke them.' Morton gave a grim smile. 'They say that cigarettes are bad for your health. If I had known the consequences of that particular illicit cigarette…'

He closed his eyes, as if willing the past back to life. 'We sat on the edge of the wood, smoking our cigarettes, laughing at the younger ones coughing and spluttering, watching the sun on the waves. And then we saw it, low on the horizon, a blaze of light, pulsing, throbbing. At first we thought it was just light glinting on some great ship in the far distance, but the closer it came, the more we realised that this was no earthly ship.'

'A spacecraft.'

Morton opened his eyes. 'It was just magnificent, Doctor, a vast disc of copper and bronze skimming over the sea. We sat watching it approach, mesmerised by its beauty, realising only far, far too late that the occupant of this magnificent machine had no control over his craft and what danger we were in.'

'It crashed?'

Morton nodded. 'We thought that it would smash into the cliff face, but at the last moment it lurched skyward, skimming the tree tops so close that I thought we would be able to reach out and touch it. We watched it arc overhead, and then it started to fall. We ran, terrified, as it smashed through the trees, the sound of tortured engines ringing in our ears. And then it exploded, throwing us all to the ground, splintering trees like toothpicks. We were lucky that day, or so we thought. We survived the explosion. If we had picked a slightly different spot for our nefarious activities…' Morton shrugged. 'Then perhaps things would have ended then and there and none of this would be necessary.'

'But things didn't end then and there, did they, Nathaniel? This story doesn't end with the explosion of a spacecraft on a remote stretch of Welsh coast, does it?'

'No, Doctor. As I said, we were young, inquisitive. We thought that the world was ours and that we were indestructible. We picked ourselves up and made our way carefully through that shattered, smouldering wood, determined to see where the saucer had crashed. You know the new estate on the hill overlooking the village?'

The Doctor nodded.

'All that was once woodland, razed by the fire from that doomed ship. The crater was vast, a great ragged gouge in the earth. Through the smoke we could see sections of the saucer: the metal, twisted and scorched, huge lumps of it, and machinery scattered as far as the eye could see. The flames were tremendous, the air like an open oven, but nonetheless we went as close as we dared, shielding our faces from the heat with our arms. It seemed impossible that anyone – or anything – could possibly have survived that terrible carnage, but we had to know.'

'And something had survived, hadn't it?' said the Doctor. 'Something alien.'

Morton met the Doctor's gaze. 'Alien and terrible. We were all straining to see into the crater when it appeared, rising up out of the flames. Huge, unimaginably powerful. It was screaming in pain, flames over every part of it, its body torn almost to pieces in the crash. The noise it made overwhelmed us. It was in our ears and in our heads, enveloping us, consuming us with its pain, its anger, its will to survive.'

Morton wiped a trembling hand across his brow.

'I staggered back from the crater, desperate to get away. My head felt as though it would burst. I could hear things, see things in my mind, terrible alien things. Ancient things from the depths of space. I could hear my cousin and the others screaming too. We were... connected somehow, sharing the death of this creature. It tried to claw its way from the crater, but the flames and its wounds were too much for it. It fell back into the wreck of its burning ship, its death throes sending me to my knees. I could feel it burning me, burning my soul. And then it stopped.'

Morton took a deep breath. 'That was the start of it, Doctor. With the death of that creature, the start of a life of torment. We hurried away from that place. Already we could hear the jangle of bells from the fire engines and people were hurrying over to see what had happened. We made a pact that night, the seven of us, never to tell of what we had seen, never to speak of it outside our group. But we left that place with more than we had arrived with. The echo of that creature was still inside our heads.'

The Doctor leaned close to Morton, peering into his eyes, his brow furrowed. 'And it's still in there, isn't it? Trapped inside you, struggling to survive, to get back out.'

'Not all of it.' Peyne stepped closer to Morton's side, running her gloved hand almost tenderly over the old man's head. 'Just a fraction, a portion of the whole.'

'Those people in the ward downstairs!' the Doctor exclaimed. 'They are the other children that witnessed the crash!'

'Each of them holding part of the mind of Balor.'

'And you've promised to remove those pieces. Well, you've been taking your time! Seventy years or more to track down seven children. Not exactly rushing things, are you?'

Peyne hissed angrily. 'We traversed sixteen star systems looking for Balor. The Brintepi had laid a trap for him on their home world, bound him with their technology and cast his ship out into space and time.'

'Ah yes, the great battle of Monson Daar. Not your finest hour.'

'The cowards made a pre-emptive strike. Massacred our defences.'

'So now you intend to bring Balor back to life.'

'Balor is the god of our people! It is written that we must free him and he will lead us to victory.'

'Careless of you to lose him, then.' The Doctor cocked his head to one side. 'So, come on. How did you find him? Doesn't sound as though he had much of a chance to send you a postcard after he crashed. And I'm assuming that everything was covered up here fairly quickly. Spacecraft crashes do tend to stir things up a little.'

Morton gave a spluttering laugh. 'Indeed. But governments had secret departments even in the 1930s, and it's extraordinary how a few threats and a lot of bribes can silence a community. The remains of the saucer vanished almost overnight, the crater was filled in and the entire incident forgotten…'

'And you and your friends?'

'Things were different back then, Doctor. Children were to be seen and not heard. No one knew what we had witnessed, no one bothered to ask beyond a cursory interview with the local policeman. We were persuaded to believe that the crash was a military aircraft, patted on the head and sent on our way. Forgotten, unimportant.'

'But with a fragment of creature still within each of you. That must have been hard.' There was sympathy in the Doctor's voice.

'Some of us coped better than others, Doctor. My

cousin spent fifteen years in an asylum; his sister was imprisoned for the attempted murder of her mother; one became a monk and never uttered a word in the rest of his life. Each of us carried a different aspect of the creature, each of us reacted to it differently, was controlled by it differently.'

'And no one realised that anything was wrong? No one tried to help you?'

'The world had other concerns, Doctor. War was looming. What were the problems of a handful of schizophrenic children when the Nazi hordes were poised to sweep across Europe? By the time I was old enough to realise the danger I was in, my mind was already being swamped by the creature within me. Balor kept me from harming myself, tried to keep all of us from succumbing to anything that could endanger the fragment of him in our minds. Even so, I doubt I would have survived the war if it had not been for the Cynrog.'

He glanced up at Peyne. 'They came for me during the Blitz. I was living in London at the time, working for a patent office, invalided out of the armed services because of my supposed "mental aberration". I thought that a bomb had landed on the house, but they had used the bombing to conceal their landing.'

Peyne gave a thin smile. 'An exhilarating flight. I had forgotten the pleasures of a simple, old-fashioned world war.'

'How did you find him?'

'Through meditation and patience. The Synod sent operatives to every corner of the universe, scanning the ether, looking for signs, scouring the psychic planes with our minds. The conflict on this planet attracted our curiosity, and it led us to discover Morton.'

'Who led you in turn to the others.' The Doctor nodded slowly. The long, sad history was now dropping into place.

'Eventually.' Peyne sighed. 'It took a long time to piece Morton's mind back together until he was of use to us. He was closest to the crash, so he holds the greatest part of Balor.'

'A lifetime's work, Doctor.' Morton sounded tired now. 'Year upon year tracking down the others, stealing them one by one from under the noses of the authorities, taking them against their will if necessary. Bringing them back here. Preparing them for this moment. Bringing them home.'

'To the rectory.'

'Yes. The crash site area holds a residual psychic trace that is beneficial to the Balor entity.'

'And keeping them in a vegetative state, that was beneficial too?'

'For the protection of Balor, yes,' snapped Peyne. 'Their primitive minds struggle with the fragments they contain. One of the females had attempted suicide. We cannot risk losing a single part of his essence before we have renewed him.'

'And *that's* what all this is about!' The Doctor waved expansively around the library. 'Renewal. Removing all the pieces of Balor back out of the minds of the children that witnessed him crash all those years ago and putting those pieces… in here!' He spun, staring up at the monster that hung before him. 'Putting them back in a great big specially constructed body. A body constructed from psychic projections, from the nightmares.'

He turned back to Peyne. 'Why? Why go to all the trouble of using the children, eh? Why not just use the memories of Morton and his friends to reconstruct the body of Balor as he was?'

'We're too old, Doctor, too weak.' Morton sighed. 'I still have some strength, but the others…'

'Besides,' Peyne said, circling the Doctor slowly, 'why stick to his old form when we could create something so much better? The children of this planet were perfect for our needs. It surprises me that the planet has survived so long. Do you know that they actively encourage their young to make war a game? Their culture is riddled with it. Toy pistols, toy rifles, toy grenades, war comics, action figures that hold knives and swords. Even when they avoid war, the young of this planet are exposed to horror comics, monsters under the bed, bogeymen, vampires and werewolves. Their nursery stories are full of demons and goblins and witches and kidnapped children. They enter the world screaming, and as soon as they can read or listen or learn they are made to scream again and again and again, before they finally realise that they have been lied to all their young lives. We didn't need to influence the minds of these children at all, Doctor, we just needed to harvest their boundless imagination.'

'Take them young, before they become tainted, is that it?' The Doctor spat the words.

'Exactly! Have you listened to the adults of this planet, listened to the endless trivia they spout? Mindless, pointless, endless conversations about nothing. They lose everything that they have as children, ground down by the reality of the world they have created. But catch them young –' Peyne turned to the creature, arms stretched wide – 'and see what they are capable of creating.'

'So you scour their dreams, sifting through their nightmares and taking the parts that suit your purpose. To create this. The ultimate body.'

'Precisely. In a few hours we will have attained full solidity, a fully functioning creature. And when it is filled with the mind of Balor…' Peyne stopped, her eyes shining with anticipation, before concluding triumphantly, 'then you will see what nightmares are really about.'

The Doctor grasped the arms of Morton's chair. 'Nathaniel, you must stop this. The Cynrog are using you. If they extract the creature from you and the others and put it inside this abomination, then nothing will stand in their way. They will be unstoppable.'

'But I want to be free of this, Doctor. Don't you see! I don't want this thing inside my head any more. I want my life back.'

'What life?' The Doctor shook his head. 'I'm sorry for you, Nathaniel, I really am, but your life has gone by. That's unfair, that's cruel, but it's the truth. You and the others have suffered more than you should have done, but you must end this, for all of you, before it's too late. You're eighty years old. You can't get your life back.'

'But I can, Doctor, that's the point…'

The Doctor stepped back from the wheelchair, eyes narrowing. 'What has she promised you, Nathaniel?'

'Renewal, Doctor. Not just for Balor, but for seven children whose lives he took. The life that was taken from us. That we deserve to have.'

'Impossible.'

'Not impossible, Doctor.' Peyne was smiling unpleasantly. 'Our machinery is capable of extracting more than just unconscious mental energy.'

'Your machinery is capable of doing lots of unpleasant things. You might be able to create an artificial life form with your psychomorphic generators, but you can't renew living tissue with it.'

'Very true.'

'That can only be done by extracting the life force.'

Peyne merely smiled.

The Doctor turned back to Morton in disgust. 'You can't condone this. Killing all those children just to save your own life?'

Morton stared, his jaw working silently, horror in his eyes. 'Peyne...'

'You didn't tell him, did you, Peyne?' The Doctor was shaking with rage. 'You didn't bother to fill him in on that particular little detail, did you? The body you are creating for Balor can be constructed from the children's imaginations, but renewing Morton and his friends, that can only be done by extracting the life force from the very same children. You can give him back his youth all right, but at the cost of the life of every child in this village!'

Morton slumped back in his chair. 'Dear God, no...'

The Doctor lunged forward at Peyne, but the gun in her hand swung up, pointing straight at the Doctor's face.

'You think I care for the lives of a few primitive children? Yes, it amuses me to give Morton his pitiful life back. He will have precious little time to come to terms with the cost of that new life before Balor destroys his world.'

A masked Cynrog technician appeared at the doorway of the library.

'Priest Commander, Technician Hadron reports that the machine is recalibrated and ready to activate on your command.'

'Excellent!' Peyne's smile widened. 'Now, Doctor, we shall finish this. The nightmares of a Time Lord will be added to those of the children and our creature will be complete. Balor has lain dormant for too long in the minds of these ungrateful savages. Our holy war still rages, and with Balor the Destroyer at our head once more victory is certain. Tonight Balor will awaken and the Cynrog will be triumphant!'

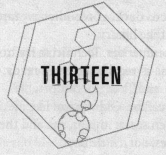

THIRTEEN

Rose pushed open the door of the ramshackle beach hut and looked cautiously around the dark and cluttered room.

'Miss Ceredig? Bronwyn?'

There was a sniff from the gloom.

'What is it? What do you want?'

'The Doctor sent me. We need your help.'

A dim light snapped on and Bronwyn's dishevelled head poked out from behind a battered old armchair. It looked to Rose as though she had been crying.

Ali peered from around the back of Rose's legs.

'Is that a duck?'

Before Rose could stop her, Ali had crossed to the sofa, perched herself on the arm and reached out a tentative hand to the imperious-looking mallard that sat there.

Bronwyn's face softened. 'His name is Butch.'

'Butch?' Ali gave her a curious look. 'That's a funny name for a duck.'

'He's a guard duck. Looks after my house when I'm out feeding the seals.'

Rose crossed to her side. 'I'm sorry to barge in, but the Doctor said you'd be able to help us.'

Bronwyn shuffled uncomfortably. 'Don't know what help I can be. Old woman like me…'

'We've been seeing things, me and the Doctor. Not just creatures, but a little boy.'

'Please, I don't know…'

'This little boy –' Rose took the picture from her pocket – 'is his name Jimmy?'

As Bronwyn took the picture, tears started to roll down her cheeks. 'Yes. My Jimmy…'

'Your son?'

Bronwyn nodded.

Rose squeezed the old woman's arm. 'It's all right. You can trust me. We want to help.'

'It was my fault. I didn't want them to take him. But they made me give him up. I couldn't stop them…'

'Who took him? Where?'

'The child protection people. They thought I was no good for him.' Bronwyn was shaking with anger and fear. 'They took him away from me once and now he's come back.' She looked at Rose with despair in her eyes. 'Nathaniel is making him come back.'

'Ow!'

The Doctor winced as the Cynrog technician pulled

the straps tight around his arms.

'Careful. I'm delicate, you know.'

The technician snarled at him and scurried away. The Doctor slumped back on to the hard bed. All around him the Cynrog were in a flurry of activity. They had abandoned their human disguises now, leaving a pile of human faces on a table. Peyne had been whipping them into a frenzy and they knew that their mission was nearly over. It was making them excitable and it was making them vicious.

They had dragged the Doctor and Morton from the library, carrying the old man bodily down the stairs and strapping him to one of the empty beds in the ward. The Doctor had had his coat and jacket removed and had been put in the bed next to him. Cynrog medical devices were strapped to both their foreheads and an intravenous drip had been thrust cruelly into the Doctor's arm. Two technicians were fussing with the connections from Morton's headset, while the old man struggled weakly.

The Doctor felt a pang of sorrow for the man. He had been strung along for years by Peyne and her colleagues, promised a new life for him and his friends, and now he was just a commodity, his use to the Cynrog nearly over.

The Doctor took a deep breath, preparing himself for the ordeal that was about to come. He hoped that his reasoning was correct with regard to the nature of the Cynrog machines. If he was wrong...

Priest Commander Peyne strode across to his bedside. She was now dressed in battle fatigues, her disrupter slung at her side.

'Ah, Miss Peyne!' The Doctor raised his head from the pillow. 'Slipped into something a bit more uncomfortable, I see. Eager to rejoin the war, I suppose.'

'The fleet is awaiting our signal. As soon as Balor has taken control of his body, we shall conduct our first battlefield test...'

'You can't unleash him on this planet, Peyne.'

She shrugged. 'An unworthy target, I agree, but it will have to serve.'

'That's not what I meant. There are billions of people here...'

'Then billions will die! The last of the Time Lords among them.' She leaned close, teeth bared. 'I hope that thought gives you nightmares, Doctor.' Then she straightened up and crossed to her technicians.

'Activate the transmitters. Full power.'

Cynrog hunched over their consoles, hands dancing over the controls. A low hum of power started to build in pitch. The Doctor felt the bands around his head crackle with power.

'Peyne, it's not too late,' he said through gritted teeth.

'But it is, Doctor. Far too late.'

Her hand slammed down on the controls.

The Doctor felt himself lift from the body strapped to the bed. Images from his past threatened to overwhelm him, memories he had fought to keep buried, memories of the time war, of the peoples he had sworn to protect. He struggled to maintain control over his thoughts and dreams, focusing his mind. The Cynrog machinery was operating on a similar frequency to the TARDIS telepathic circuits; the fact that Rose's dreams had been affected while they were still in flight proved that. His own link to the TARDIS meant that he should be able to use that power, channel it, turn it back on itself...

Blackness swirled around him, dark shapes flitting through the shadows, nightmares from his distant childhood. He forced himself to ignore them. There were other minds in the ether with him, belonging to Morton and the six sleepers. He could feel the human parts of them struggling to be free of the powerful influence of Balor, sense their relief as the alien that had inhabited their minds for so long was slowly drawn out.

Balor was terrifyingly strong. The Doctor could sense the ancient force that the Cynrog sought to harvest. But something was not right. The creature was savage, primal, but unfinished somehow, unfocused, as if some part of it was missing, some controlling part that would bring order to the whole.

The Doctor could feel the Cynrog machines probing at his memories, trying to force their way into the darkest fears. He shut down sections of his mind, erecting psychic barriers that would keep the Cynrog out. He hoped…

The power started to increase and he struggled to retain control.

'Hello.'

The voice was shocking and loud. The Doctor could hear it all around him.

A small child stood next to him, staring down at the body that lay on the bed. It was the child the Doctor had seen earlier in the woods and on the island. The child Rose had seen in her dream.

'Hello. It's Jimmy, isn't it?'

The boy nodded, a frown on his small face. 'I think so. I used to be. I think I might be something else now. I'm how she remembers me, before they took her away from me.'

The Doctor winced at the child's directness.

'They took you away?'

'They said she was a bad mother. That she couldn't look after me properly. The monster made her different. The monster in her head. I can feel it in my head too. It's not very nice.'

The Doctor's mind raced. 'This monster,' he asked, 'has it been in her head a long time?'

The boy nodded again. 'She saw it when she was small. She was hiding from the others and she saw it. It hid a bit of itself in her head. It made her do bad things.'

'Can you show me, show me that memory?'

'I think so. Mummy's memories are so muddled these days.'

The little boy took his hand and the Doctor felt a jolt of surprise at the solidness of the touch. He now knew where the controlling part of Balor's mind was, the intelligence, the dangerous heart.

They swept through a dizzying array of images and thoughts, searching for one tiny memory, the shared memory of that terrible day when Balor's crippled spacecraft had roared over the sea and crashed at Ynys Du.

On the edge of his consciousness he could feel something building, something powerful and vast. Balor, waking from his rest, aware of this child by his side. He concentrated, pushing past the monsters of the children, forcing his way into the minds of Morton and the others, willing them to remember.

There! The memory he searched for flickered into life: frightened children clustered around a burning spacecraft, terrified and exhilarated at the same time. The Doctor felt their fear as Balor crawled his way out of the pit, a mass of flames and fury, felt their pain and confusion as his mind seared into theirs…

The cold touch of death swept over him and, with a chill, the Doctor realised that he was experiencing Balor's fractured memory too. He felt the rage and anger of the creature, its unmitigated hatred, its thrill when a world was crushed in its grasp, its final desperate fight to cling to existence, reaching out to whatever lifeline it could find...

'There she is.'

Jimmy was pointing at the hidden observer who crouched on the far side of the crater, unseen by the children but noticed by Balor.

The Doctor stared at the eighth child as she watched the creature's fiery death, a child whose face he'd seen in photographs earlier in the day. Bronwyn. Her auburn hair and silver-grey eyes were unmistakable. From the other side of crater, she watched in horror as the creature burned, clutching at her head as it poured its mind into her.

The residual psychic echo that the Cynrog had detected wasn't from the crash site. It was from Bronwyn.

Which meant that the Cynrog didn't have all the pieces of Balor's psyche. Bronwyn still held the vital missing fragment.

In the pub Beth was looking round in horror as children started to drop where they stood. Frantic parents were desperately trying to shake them awake again, but it was hopeless. The youngest were going first, falling into a deep, deep sleep.

Outside the roaring of monsters started again.

Beth clamped her hands over her ears.

'He's failed. The Doctor's failed!'

'Rose!'

'Doctor?'

Rose sprang to her feet, looking around Bronwyn's ramshackle house, surprised by the Doctor's voice. Apart from Bronwyn, Ali and Butch the room was empty. She turned in a slow circle, puzzled.

'Where are you?'

'Strapped to a bed in the rectory. Don't ask stupid questions!'

Realisation dawned on Rose. 'Are you in my head? Are you poking around inside my head with telepathy or something?'

'Yes! Now listen.'

'I don't believe this! Aren't you meant to ask or anything before you come barging in?'

'Rose, I *really* don't have too much time! The Cynrog got inside your dreams because their machinery operates on the same frequency that the TARDIS uses to translate languages in your head. I'm hitching a ride on the same frequencies because they've wired me into their system. They're occupied at the moment and I'm cleverer than they are, but it's taking a lot of effort and I don't have much time so I need you to shut up and listen.'

Rose sat down hard, aware of the curious looks she was getting from the others. Presumably they were only hearing one side of the conversation.

'OK, I'm listening,' she whispered.

'Right. And don't talk, just think. Think the words.'

Rose gritted her teeth and concentrated on forming the words in her head. 'All right.'

'Good. I know what the connection between Bronwyn and the boy is.'

'Yeah. He's her son. And you were right, his name's Jimmy.'

'I'm having a chat with him now. At least, I'm with something that looks like him, something that has his memories, but it probably has a good part of something else too.'

'Hang about… You're with him? But they sent him away. He got adopted. It nearly finished her. Ended her marriage. It was when he was small, but that was years ago. She doesn't even know if he's still alive.'

'Yeah, well, this one is still about six.'

'OK, this is getting seriously creepy.'

She realised that she had said this out loud when Ali gave her a puzzled look. Smiling embarrassedly, she forced herself to concentrate on her thoughts again.

'She blames herself. Says she was a bad mother. That she's been keeping something secret all these years, in her head. I think that's what's made her a bit, you know... odd.'

'Yes, well, she's got a fair chunk of an alien lodged in her brain, and not a nice one either. Must have been affecting her for years.'

'You what?'

'Doesn't matter. All you need to know is that she's got something the Cynrog don't know about. Let's keep it that way. Will she take you to the lighthouse?'

'Yeah. She's just sorting out a lifejacket for Ali.'

'Right. You're gonna have to hurry, 'cause things are going to start prowling again shortly. And there's a bit of a change with what I want you to do. Still got the sonic screwdriver?'

'Of course.'

'OK, then listen carefully.'

The eyes of the creature in the library flickered open. This time they weren't dead and unseeing, but blazed with angry life. It examined its surroundings, straining at the energy field that held it suspended in the charged air.

The energy waves that rolled across its skin had faded now and the flesh of the creature was solid and real. Hard, chitinous plates covered its back and arms, studded with wickedly barbed spines. Its back was hunched and muscular, the thick neck wreathed with writhing tentacles. Its head was flat and elongated, the brain protected by a hard, bony plate flaring out to an armoured frill, like a dinosaur. The black eyes blazed from beneath a heavy brow and row upon row of curving teeth gnashed in the wide mouth. Six powerful insect-like legs flexed under its abdomen, the claws at their tips gleaming and sharpened, and curling over its back was a segmented, scorpion-like tail, poison dripping from the spines that studded its length.

The creature gave a bellow of anger at its confinement, lashing out with a clawed hand. Cynrog equipment shattered under the blow, tendrils of energy arcing angrily across the library. Enraged by the lightning, the creature started to lash out blindly, tearing the cables from the walls, sending books and consoles crashing to the ground.

With a huge shower of sparks, the Cynrog machinery exploded, energy dancing wildly across the room, spitting flames in its wake. The creature crashed to the floor, released from the energy field. Its claws took huge gouges from the polished floorboards as it spread its arms wide and let out a shattering roar.

Peyne looked up as the roar reverberated around the house.

'Balor,' she whispered.

The Cynrog technicians had stopped their work at the consoles, looking at each other in excitement. The ward was filled with reptilian hissing.

'Back to your stations!' barked Peyne. 'Priest Technician Hadron, with me!'

The two Cynrog marched from the room, throwing open the doors to the hallway. From upstairs came another mighty roar, coupled with the dull crump of explosions. Smoke was starting to fill the house, billowing across the once ornate ceilings.

Peyne frowned. 'Something is not right.'

As they raced up the stairs, lithe and lizard-like, Peyne's heart was pounding. To fail when they were this close...

They skidded to a halt outside the library, staring in shock at the devastation that faced them. The heavy wooden doors had burst from their hinges, leaving huge, jagged splinters scattered across the floor. Chunks of plaster had been torn from the walls and ceiling and thick black smoke billowed out into the corridor. Another explosion shot gouts of flame through the open doorway, sending the Cynrog diving for cover.

Through the flames Peyne could see something moving. Something huge and dark. Hadron fumbled with the disrupter at his belt.

Peyne hissed angrily at him, 'Fool! You think we've come this far just for you to shoot him down? Conduct yourself as befits a Priest Technician of the Cynrog.'

Hadron bowed his head. 'My apologies, Priest Commander.'

Peyne flicked her tongue in displeasure and smoothed down the creases in her battle fatigues. She would have preferred full ceremonial regalia for this moment, the end of so many years of waiting.

Head held high, she entered the library, Hadron at her side.

'Lord Balor, we of the Cynrog rejoice at your coming. Lead us once more to the victory…'

The words died in her throat as the creature turned slowly to face her. She felt her skin prickle, the spines across her scalp stiffening in fear. Her hands were shaking; the creature was using its power on them.

'My Lord Balor?'

Peyne stared up into the face of the towering monster, into the blazing eyes that were fixed on her, and at that moment she knew that something had gone terribly, horribly wrong. Instinctively she realised that the creature in front of her was incomplete. Somehow, something was missing. Somehow, *she* had missed something, and the thing that she had created was a savage, indiscriminate, uncontrolled animal. The soul that inhabited it had only one thought: destruction.

The creature opened its wide mouth and let out a growl of hatred.

'Commander…' Hadron had dropped to his knees, his body shaking uncontrollably.

The monster lifted a huge claw.

'No!'

Peyne threw herself backwards as the claw slashed down, swiping Hadron into the air. She could hear the screams of the technician as the huge jaws closed around his torso, the wet crunch as the creature devoured him.

Balor gave another deafening roar and raised himself to his full height. Wooden beams strained and splintered, and plaster shattered like glass as the monster burst up through the roof of the rectory. Cold air swept in, fanning the flames that leapt from the devastated equipment and now raged across the ancient bookcases. Masonry tumbled into the room as a chimneystack was torn apart by the struggling monster.

Peyne scrambled to her feet and ran for her life.

Rose struggled up the wet rocks to the base of the lighthouse with Ali lolling in her arms. She had to keep shaking the little girl to keep her awake.

'Come on, Ali. Come on! We're nearly there. Two more minutes and this will all be over. Two more minutes.'

'I'm so tired, Rose.' Ali rubbed at her eyes.

'I know, honey, I know, but I need you. Try to keep going just a bit longer, please. For me.'

Ali nodded weakly.

Rose turned to see where Bronwyn had got to. The

old woman was picking her way painfully up the slope. The ride across to the island had been terrifying. The monsters had started to emerge again, in ones and twos at first, but then things had started to flash through the water around the little boat and Rose hadn't been sure if they would ever get here in one piece.

When Ali had started to flag, at first Rose thought it was just due to the rigours of the day, but now it seemed certain that she was falling victim to the Cynrog machines once more.

'Bronwyn, I've got to get Ali to the lamp room. Are you OK?'

'Got to rest. Got to sit.' Her words came between rasping breaths. 'So tired.'

'Not you too!'

Rose groaned. She couldn't keep both of them awake for ever, but at least the cold rain was helping. She looked up at the lighthouse. The glow from the lamp room above them was lighting up the storm clouds. She pushed open the metal door, ushering Bronwyn inside.

'OK. You stay here. I'll be as quick as I can.'

'You go on, dear.' Bronwyn waved a weary hand at Rose. 'I'm getting too old for all this running about.' She lowered herself on to the bottom step of the winding staircase. 'I'll just sit here for a while.'

With a last worried look at the slumped old lady at her feet, Rose hefted Ali in her arms and started up the stairs, her legs protesting at every step.

She reached the lamp room breathless, her heart threatening to burst out of her chest. Lowering Ali to the floor, she fumbled in her pocket for the sonic screwdriver, then pressed it into the little girl's hand.

'You remember what you have to do?'

'I think so.'

Ali looked fearfully into the glowing room, the green light pulsating and throbbing. Rose hugged her hard.

'You can do this. I know you can.'

Ali took a deep breath, gave Rose a wavering smile and stepped into the lamp room.

Peyne tore the sensors from the Doctor's brow, hurling them across the ward.

'What have you done, Time Lord?' she snarled.

The Doctor's eyes flickered open. 'Morning already?'

Peyne hauled him upright, digging her claws into the flesh of his arms. 'I said what have you done?'

She flinched as a mass of bricks and timber crashed into the hallway outside the door. A guttural bellow rang out from somewhere upstairs.

'Oh dear.' The Doctor gave a huge grin. 'It does sound as though you've got a few problems, doesn't it? Our Lord Balor got out of the wrong side of the bed, did he?'

Peyne dragged the Doctor from his own bed,

pressing her disrupter to his temples.

'For the last time, Doctor, tell me what you have done!' she roared.

'Nothing!' The Doctor slapped the gun away angrily. 'I've done nothing, Peyne. This is your doing. Fifty years to get this right and you still messed it up!'

'What do you mean?'

Peyne's eyes narrowed, her flattened nose wrinkling in anger. Around her the Cynrog looked at each other in concern, confused and frightened.

'You didn't do your job properly, that's what I mean! Priest Commander of the Cynrog?' The Doctor gave a snort of derision. 'No wonder your pitiful little race never gets anywhere!'

He crossed to one of the nervous technicians. 'Gonna take orders from a commander who can't even count, hm? From someone who thinks that she's such a clever clogs because she found a way of using the local kids as a resource but didn't make sure she had all the facts.'

He dodged out of the way as a lump of plaster crashed down from the ceiling.

'You've made a lovely big monster with huge pointy teeth, but it's not got all its marbles, has it? You missed a bit, thicko!'

'Another child,' breathed Peyne.

'Yes, another child. Another poor wretch who spent the best years of her life with a fragment of your god inside her head!' The Doctor's voice was cold, hard. 'And now you've unleashed your creature without checking that it's in its right mind, a creature that is mentally unbalanced, unfinished, uncontrollable! All you've done is created another nightmare. You've failed, Peyne!'

'NO!' Peyne screamed in frustration and anger. She stumbled across to one of the humming consoles, pushing her milling technicians aside, claws dancing across controls. 'It's not too late. We can still find the child.'

'It took you fifty years to find the others! What chance do you have of finding another one now?'

'Because she's close, Doctor. Here somewhere. See. The readings are almost at optimum. Almost! That means the child is close, within range of the receptors! I'm not going to fail!' She spat the words. 'Not now! I'm not going to have wasted my time on this miserable planet.'

'Your creature will have burnt itself out long before you have time to complete the transfer, Peyne. Listen to it. It's tearing itself apart!'

'Then perhaps we need to give it some self-control.'

Peyne started stabbing at buttons and energy flickered around the heads of Morton and the others in the beds. Old bodies twisted in pain, backs arching.

'What are you doing?'

'Nathaniel Morton and his friends can perform one

final service in the Cynrog cause. Their minds are weak, but they can still serve to calm the creature, just long enough for me to find this one last fragment.'

'No!'

The Doctor tried to pull Peyne away from the controls. She thrust him back savagely, whipping the disrupter from her pocket.

'You've become expendable, Doctor.'

She pulled the trigger.

Ali lay flat on her stomach, stretched out under the crackling Cynrog machine. She flinched as fingers of glowing energy danced across her skin. It tingled. Her eyes were getting heavier and heavier; the sonic screwdriver felt like a lump of lead in her hand.

'Don't stop, Ali.'

She could hear Rose shouting from the door.

'Remember what I told you!'

Ali struggled to concentrate. Ahead of her she could see the cluster of black nodules that she had to reach. She shuffled forward on her tummy. There. She could reach them now. So what was it she had to do?

She yawned. She was so tired and it was warm here under the machine. Warm and glowing. She rested her head on her arm. A few moments wouldn't hurt.

'No! Ali, don't!'

Rose was banging on the metal floor. Ali could feel the vibrations.

'All right, all right!'

She struggled to lift the sonic screwdriver, holding the tip against the first nodule. There was a harsh blue light and a piercing whine and the back lump split open, revealing a single dial. Ali reached out and turned it from 'three o'clock' to 'two o'clock', as she had been told. The hum from the machine above changed in pitch.

Ali moved to the next nodule. Six more to go.

At the bottom of the lighthouse Bronwyn peered out through the open doorway and smiled at the small figure that wandered towards her from the beach.

She was so very tired. Perhaps it was time to stop, to finally give up.

Inside her head she could feel the thing that she had carried since her childhood struggling to be free. Perhaps it was time to let go.

She leaned back on the steps, surrendering to unconsciousness.

The wall of the house collapsed just as the disrupter went off. Bricks slammed into Peyne's arm, knocking the gun aside and sending the disrupter bolt ricocheting across the room. Peyne grasped her arm in agony, watching in disbelief as one wall bulged outwards, collapsing in a heap into the once neat gardens.

Cynrog scattered as beams and plaster rained down among them, smashing machinery.

The Doctor darted out through the gaping hole and into the rain, ducking inside the porch and staring up at the rectory.

'Now there's something you don't see every day.'

The huge Balor creature was on the roof, legs skittering on the wet tiles. The last vestiges of energy from the Cynrog generators flickered around its feet. As the energy field died, the creature seemed to bulge and change, increasing in size, towering over the house. Slashing claws tore huge lumps of masonry from the building and sent them crashing to the floor. Fire had caught hold of the old timbers and one wing of the house was now ablaze, smoke billowing into the night sky, lighting the clouds with a bright orange glow.

Cynrog technicians fled from the burning house. The monster reached out with huge clawed hands and swept them up into the air, stabbing at them with its barbed tail, tearing them to pieces with its pincers. Casting the shredded bodies aside, it clambered down from the shattered roof, its movements slow and menacing, its claws digging into the stone as it clicked and clattered on to the wet lawn.

The Doctor started to back away. With a screech of pain and anger, the creature's head swung down to look at him. The Doctor swallowed hard.

'Now might be a good time to finish that little errand I sent you on, Rose,' he muttered.

'Yes, Lord Balor. Destroy him!'

Peyne emerged from the shattered dining room, her uniform ripped, a huge bloody gash in her scalp.

'Destroy the enemies of Cynrog!'

The creature turned slowly towards her, teeth bared. Peyne took a step backwards.

'My Lord, I am not your enemy! I have given you the minds of the primitives that once housed you and the final part of you is close by. Please, I beg you, control yourself. Use the primitive minds to focus. Remember who you were, who you are…'

'Peyne…'

The voice was low and guttural, rattling the windows. The Doctor could feel it vibrating in his gut.

'I… remember you… Peyne…'

'My Lord!' Peyne dropped to her knees. 'You live!'

'I remember your lies, your deceit. The years treating me like a child…'

Peyne raised her head, her eyes wide with disbelief. 'Morton?'

'Is this what I lived for, Peyne, to be your creature, your weapon? To plunder the universe, destroying and killing.'

'My Lord, the primitive mind… It is stronger than I had thought. It has some control. I…'

'Another mistake, Peyne?' The thing laughed. A

horrible, bubbling cackle. 'If this is the life you offer, so be it. If I cannot live as Nathaniel Morton the man, then I shall be Morton the Destroyer, the new god of the Cynrog... And you will serve me!'

Peyne clambered to her feet, eyes blazing with anger. 'Never.'

'As you wish.'

The Morton creature lunged forward, taking Peyne's head off with a single bite. The body stood for a few seconds, yellow ichor fountaining from its neck, then it collapsed in a crumpled heap.

The creature threw its head back and bellowed in triumph. Flexing its claws, it reared back, towering over the house, staring down at the Time Lord standing in the centre of the lawn.

'And now for you, Doctor.'

Ali reached for the final switch. With every nodule she had opened her tiredness had started to leave her. She felt more alive than she had in months. She stretched out, grasped the ridged dial and turned it. It moved with a sharp click and the machine changed in pitch once more.

'I've done it, Rose! I've done it!'

She wriggled out from under the machine, sonic screwdriver held proudly in her hands.

Her smile turned to disappointment. Rose was fast asleep.

* * *

Behind the bar of the Red Lion Beth Hardy watched as her husband slumped down across the table he was clearing, dead to the world. She barely had enough time to put a full glass of bitter on the bar top before she too collapsed in a heap.

Across the village children woke from their nightmares and watched in disbelief as their parents slumped back in chairs and on to carpets as sleep overtook them.

The village of Ynys Du reverberated to the sounds of heavy snoring.

The Doctor closed his eyes as the razor claws reached out through the rain, waiting for the killer blow.

It never came.

He opened one eye cautiously.

The creature was staring at its claws, turning them this way and that. It looked down at the Doctor.

'I think I chipped a nail.'

The Doctor blinked. 'I'm sorry?'

'A nail. Look.' It held out a claw. 'And that head. Do you think it's going to be fattening? You never know with foreign food, do you?'

The creature skittered across the lawn, staring at its reflection in the tall windows of the rectory. 'Do you think I look all right in this? I'm not sure if it suits me. I'm meant to be going to Maureen's wedding next week and I'm really not convinced.'

As the Doctor watched, a flicker of energy lanced from the roof of the shattered rectory and danced around the creature's outline. Balor seemed to be shrinking.

It started to scamper in circles, arms waving agitatedly. 'Oh, God. I'm not sure I'm going to be able to make that mortgage payment in time. And what if I don't get that job at the chemist? He says he wants to settle down, but I know he's still seeing Pauline from the WH Smith in town. Three of Dai Williams's chickens dropped dead last week. I hope we've not got that bird flu thing here...'

The creature was shrinking faster and faster now, its scales fading, changing, its skin becoming pinstriped, masked, different football colours, a blur of shapes and images. The voice got more and more frantic, words blurring into each other. The Doctor could hear snatches of half-shouted fears: global warming, old age, cellulite, rent cheques, girlfriends, boyfriends, debts, affairs.

The creature was a whirling blur now. And then, with a sudden pop, it vanished.

The Doctor stood in the rain in the middle of the lawn, staring at the spot where the creature had been. Choking clouds of black smoke billowed into the night air as more and more of the rectory succumbed to the flames.

A shattering explosion sent him tumbling across the

grass. That was presumably the last of the Cynrog machinery.

He picked himself up and glanced across to the wreckage of the dining room. That room too was ablaze. The husks of those people who had held the mind of Balor for most of their lives were finally free.

The last of the Cynrog technicians were rushing about in confusion. The Doctor sighed. He had work to do. He couldn't let desperate aliens wander free.

He clapped his hands. 'Right, you lot. Your commander's dead, your god is gone, I'm the rightful guardian of this planet and it's time for you to sling your hook, before I get *really* angry.'

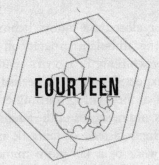

FOURTEEN

The young woman lay peacefully on the stretcher, blankets tucked protectively around her. The Doctor brushed a strand of auburn hair gently from her forehead.

The woman's eyelids flickered open briefly to reveal sparkling grey eyes. The Doctor smiled at her. She caught hold of his hand and squeezed it.

'Thank you,' Bronwyn whispered. 'For setting me free.'

The Doctor shook his head. 'Your boy set you free. Your Jimmy. He showed me what you had seen. What I needed to do.'

Bronwyn smiled. 'He was such a good boy.'

'Who loved his mother. Always.'

A hurrying paramedic manoeuvred the Doctor firmly to one side, catching hold of the stretcher's handles. His colleague took the other end and they hoisted Bronwyn off the beach and into the waiting ambulance.

The Doctor closed the doors behind them and watched as the ambulance roared off through the village, lights whirling. Bronwyn's rejuvenation had been an unexpected bonus. As he had hoped, Ali's readjustment of the Cynrog transmitters had tapped into the fears and neuroses of the adults of Ynys Du, not the children. Instead of fantastic monsters, the nightmares were of a far more mundane nature. 'Tainted by the trivia of the real world,' as Peyne had put it. Without the imagination of the children to sustain it, the monster had simply ceased to exist.

He glanced up at the smudge of grey smoke that trailed into the blue sky from the cliff top. The fire in the rectory had raged all night. There would be no traces of the Cynrog machinery by now.

He crossed to where Rose sat on the sea wall, shaking her head in disbelief. Ali was perched next to her.

'I just came down the stairs and she was sitting there, fast asleep.'

'How did old Bronwyn become pretty again?'

Ali had her head cocked to one side, squinting at the Doctor.

He tried to look casual. 'Well, the Cynrog transmitters were still working flat out until the moment they blew up. As soon as the monster was finally solid, they were designed to switch frequencies and suck the life force out of you lot to rejuvenate Mr

Morton and his friends. When Peyne started to triangulate on Bronwyn's psychic signature, looking for the final piece of Balor, the machinery somehow got its polarity reversed. Instead of rejuvenating Morton and the others, it took *their* life force and rejuvenated Bronwyn instead.'

Ali frowned and nudged Rose. 'Does he always talk like that or do you get him to speak English sometimes?'

Rose laughed. 'Nah, he's always like this.'

'Of course, the machinery was also operating on similar frequencies to the TARDIS, so there's a possibility that she had a hand in it somewhere…'

'The TARDIS…' Rose looked at him quizzically.

'Yeah, well, she does like to… interfere sometimes.'

'Right. I wonder where she gets that from.'

'I'll tell you another thing…' The Doctor hopped up on to the wall next to Rose, whispering into her ear. 'Bronwyn's pregnant.'

'No way? Another Jimmy?'

'Could be.'

'But isn't everything gonna just start up all over again? Doesn't she still have a bit of that Balor thing inside her mind?'

'Not any more.' The Doctor tapped the side of his head. 'In here. Ooh, nasty little bit it is, all buzzy and angry like a big wasp. Gonna have to give myself a mental enema when we get back to the TARDIS.'

'Eeergh!' Rose and Ali both grimaced.

'Come on, Ali!' The Doctor bounded off the wall, catching her by the hands. 'Rose and I have got equipment to strip out of a lighthouse and some Cynrog to send on their way, and I want to buy you an ice cream before we go.'

Dai Barraclough puffed and panted as he took the final few steps on to the cliff top.

'What have you dragged us all the way up here for, Hardy?'

Ali glared at him. 'I told you. I've got something special to show you.'

'It'd better be worth it.'

'Shut up, Dai.' Billy Palmer threw him an angry glare. 'If Ali says it's special, then it'll be special.'

Ali smiled at him. She liked Billy Palmer.

The rest of the gang were squatted down on the grass at the cliff edge, staring out at the jagged rocks of Black Island. The sun was high in the sky, sending silver highlights dancing over the waves. A fresh breeze blew in from the sea, swaying the tall grass and flecking the rocks far below with foam.

'What are we looking for, Ali?' asked one of the twins.

Ali glanced at her watch. 'You'll see. Any moment now...'

With a loud rumble, something emerged from

behind the lighthouse in a blaze of light, a silver shape skimming over the water before lifting higher and higher into the blue sky.

The children watched open-mouthed as it curved above them and then, with a flare of dazzling light, streaked away towards the horizon, the roar of its engines sending seagulls shrieking into the brilliant blue.

Ali shielded her eyes from the sun and smiled.

The Doctor and Rose stood in the console room of the TARDIS, eating their ice cream cones, watching on the scanner screen as the silver shape of the Cynrog ship slowly made its way out of orbit, accelerating away from the Earth.

'You've sent them back to their war, then?' Rose sounded disapproving.

'Yeah, but by the scenic route.'

'How scenic?'

'Oh… about…. forty or fifty parsecs out of their way. Should take them a couple of years at that speed.'

'A couple of years.' Rose looked shocked. 'Can they survive that long in that sardine tin?'

'Course they can! Lovely little stasis capsules in that thing. They'll sleep all the way home! Mind you…' He tailed off.

'What?'

'They might have a few bad dreams on the way.'

'Dreams?' Rose raised a quizzical eyebrow.

'Well, nightmares if you want to be strictly accurate. Just enough to ensure that they won't fancy coming back.'

'Oh yeah, and what do creatures like the Cynrog have nightmares about?'

The Doctor just smiled.

Acknowledgements

Grateful thanks are due to Justin, my editor, for refusing to take no for an answer and for endless encouragement and problem-solving during the writing of this book. And to Ian Grutchfield for convincing me that saying yes was the right thing to do. Thanks also to the usual suspects, who kept me sane during the process:

Karen Parks (x)

Sue Cowley and Steve Roberts (and their pussy cat)

Steve Cole (for belly-dancing)

Moogie and Andy Tucker (Baz lives again!)

Robert Perry (where are you?)

The Boys from the Model Unit (for Beers, Badgers and BAFTAs)

Soph and Sylv (without whom…)

and

Christopher, David and Billie (for bringing it back for a new generation).

About the Author

Mike Tucker is a visual effects designer who, after twenty years at the BBC, now runs his own company, The Model Unit, out of Ealing Studios. Having worked as an effects assistant on the original series of *Doctor Who*, he has been the Miniature Effects Supervisor on the first two seasons of the new series, overseeing the team responsible for (among other things) the destruction of Big Ben, the Daleks (and their Emperor) and K-9.

His previous books for the BBC have mostly been written with long-time colleague Robert Perry and have all revolved around the characters of the seventh Doctor and Ace. This is his first full-length novel for a different Doctor/companion team. One day he'd love to write a Dalek novel. Please...

DOCTOR · WHO

Aliens and Enemies
By Justin Richards

ISBN-10 0 563 48632 5
ISBN-13 978 0 563 48646 6
UK £7.99 US $12.99/$15.99 CDN

The Cybermen are back to terrorise time and space – but luckily the new Doctor, played by David Tennant, and Rose are back to stop them.

Picking up where Monsters and Villains left off, this fully illustrated guide documents the return of these metal menaces, as well as the Sycorax and other foes from the new series, plus first series terrors like the Gelth and the Reapers.

More classic baddies such as the dreaded Zarbi, Sutekh and the Robots of Death also make a welcome appearance.

The Art of Destruction
By Stephen Cole

ISBN-10 0 563 48651 1

ISBN-13 978 0 563 48651 0

UK £6.99 US $11.99/$14.99 CDN

The TARDIS lands in 22nd-century Africa in the shadow of a dormant volcano. Agri-teams are growing new foodstuffs in the baking soil to help feed the world's starving millions – but the Doctor and Rose have detected an alien signal somewhere close by.

When a nightmare force starts surging along the dark volcanic tunnels, the Doctor realises an ancient trap has been sprung. But who was it meant for? And what is the secret of the eerie statues that stand at the heart of the volcano?

Dragged into a centuries-old conflict, Rose and the Doctor have to fight for their lives as alien hands practice the arts of destruction all around them.

The Price of Paradise
By Colin Brake
ISBN-10 0 563 48652 X
ISBN-13 978 0 563 48652 7
UK £6.99 US $11.99/$14.99 CDN

Laylora – the Paradise Planet. A world of breath-taking beauty, where peace-loving inhabitants live in harmony with their environment. Or do they? The Doctor and Rose arrive to find that the once perfect eco-system is showing signs of failing. The paradise planet has become a death trap as terrifying creatures from ancient legends appear and stalk the land.

Is there a connection between the human explorers who have crash-landed and the savage monsters? And what price might one human have to pay to save the only home he has ever known?

The Doctor and Rose are in a race against time to find a cure for a sick planet.